A NOT SO QUIET CHRISTMAS

SUZIE TULLETT

www.bloodhoundbooks.com

Print ISBN 978-1-914614-47-7

ALSO BY SUZIE TULLETT

The Trouble With Words

Little White Lies and Butterflies

The French Escape

Six Steps To Happiness

Holly's Christmas Countdown

For Adam and Benjamin
I couldn't be prouder

CHAPTER 1

Three weeks to Christmas

I shivered as I let myself into Jules's flat, relieved to be getting out of the cold. In all my thirty-four years I'd never been a fan of winter and already looked forward to the advent of spring. "It's only me," I called out, as Frank, the dog, raced down the hall to greet me. The sight of his wagging tail, big floppy ears, and stumpy legs, brought a smile to my face. "Hello, boy," I said. I watched him dig his feet in to stop, but, as usual when it came to Frank and smooth surfaces, it was too little, too late. I made my way into the lounge and the poor thing slid straight past me.

I popped the key Jules had given me into my handbag with one hand, while carrying a potted plant in the other. Knowing how fed up she had to be, I fixed a smile on my face as I entered the room, determined to lift her spirits. "For you," I said, holding out my gift.

Stuck in her seat, my friend chuckled, looking surprisingly

content under the circumstances. "A cactus?" she said, clearly amused by my choice of gift.

"A Christmas cactus to be precise," I replied, nodding for her to take it. "Or, as the woman in the florist called it, *Schlumbergera bridgesii.*"

Frank plonked himself down on the rug while Jules admired her plant. "Thank you," she said. "It's..." My friend pondered a moment, as if trying to find the right word. "Interesting." She placed it to one side.

"You seem chirpy, considering." I took off my gloves and stuffed them into my coat pockets. "I thought you'd be weeping into your cushion by now." Jules had never been one to sit still, even more so at Christmas. Whereas I had what she called an aversion to all things festive, Jules loved the excitement of running around here, there and everywhere, organising the perfect Yuletide. Finding herself not just housebound but chair-bound, and for longer than anticipated, prevented her from doing that. I'd expected her to be devastated, not sitting there with a smile on her face.

"Unlike me," Jules said, "you've never experienced the delights of daytime television. Thanks to shows like this..." she gestured to the TV, "I now know how to bake the perfect plum pudding, choose the ideal party dress according to my shape and size, and can solve a nine-letter festive-themed conundrum in under sixty seconds." She picked up the remote and turned off her latest viewing choice. "Later this afternoon, I'll be learning how to turn someone's trash into treasure. You get the gist? Making a light fitting out of an old bicycle. That kind of thing."

I giggled at Jules's enthusiasm. "So I needn't have wasted my money on these, then?" I said.

As I reached into my bag and pulled out a box of chocolates, my friend's face broke into a grin. "Now we're talking," she replied, keener on my second offering than my first.

While Jules tore into the chocolates, I took in her leg which lay propped up on the coffee table. I could almost feel the weight of the huge, thick plaster cast that stretched from her toes to her thigh. I took off my hat and scarf and tossed them over the back of the sofa before plonking myself down. "Did they say how much longer it would be on for?"

"Your guess is as good as mine. In layman's terms the tibia and fibula aren't knitting properly. I have to go back in a couple of weeks. The orthopaedist will take it from there." She stuffed an orange cream into her mouth.

"Maybe next time you'll switch the light on when you put the rubbish out," I said.

"How was I supposed to know how icy it would be? Anyway, from now on, Harry's on bin duty." Jules grimaced. "It's one thing to go flying like I did, but I can still hear the snapping sound when my leg twisted."

I automatically reached down and rubbed the top of my shin, cringing at the thought.

Jules, however, appeared oblivious to my discomfort and quickly moved the conversation on. "Coffee?" she asked, matter of fact.

Watching her reach down the side of her chair and produce a flask and then two mugs, I couldn't help but smile. "Good to know Harry's taking care of you," I said. "Making sure you have everything you need."

"Honestly, he's been an angel. Do you know how many times that man has helped me to the bathroom? Using these..." She pointed to a pair of crutches. "I can't even pull down my own knickers."

Doing my best to shake the image she'd just conjured, I

glanced around. "Where is he, by the way?" He usually popped his head into the room to say hello when I called in.

"At the office. He's gone to pick up some files."

She poured us both a drink and while I sipped on mine, Jules proceeded to glug. "You might want to slow down with that," I said. Happy to help in most respects, there were some jobs Harry could keep. "I thought he'd taken time off?"

"He had. But seeing as we're stuck at home for the foreseeable, there's no point in him wasting his leave." Jules indicated her leg. "That's the worst part of all this. Having to postpone our trip."

Another reason why Jules deserved my sympathy, she had a lot to sort out following her aunt's death.

"I was really looking forward to getting away. To spending Christmas not just in the snow, but in proper snow. Do you know how long it's been since we had a holiday?"

No matter what life threw at her, Jules had always had the ability to put a positive slant on things. But even she had to know that seeing their trip as a vacation was a stretch too far. "Jules, sorting out your dead aunt's house isn't the same as going on a jolly."

"Every cloud and all that..."

I stared at her incredulously.

"What?" Jules let out a laugh. "It's not as if Aunt Lillian didn't have a good innings. The woman was well into her nineties and had had a fantastic life. To be honest, I'm surprised she left the house to me at all. I fully expected it to go to some weird dog sledding charity or bumblebee conservation trust. She was a bit like you that way."

"Meaning?"

"How shall I put it?" She reached down and produced the cactus. "Unconventional."

I supposed she had a point.

Jules's eyes lit up. "I used to love going to visit and not just because Aunt Lillian was so much fun. Did I ever tell you about Jason? One of Little Leatherington's local boys?"

I shrugged. Being honest, I couldn't remember one way or the other.

"Good-looking, had a bit of a reputation, you know the type. He certainly got my hormones going." She came over all dreamy. "I wonder what ever happened to him?" She shook herself back into the room. "I thought maybe I'd find out at the funeral. But thanks to this," Jules nodded to her plaster cast, "it's not like I got the chance."

"I'm sure you'll find out once you're on your feet and running again."

"That's the problem. We could do with getting things sorted sooner rather than later. We haven't a clue what to do with the place long term and thought we might get a tenant in while we decide. The local letting agent said Little Leatherington's a popular village and there are so few rentals available. Once the house is empty and has had a bit of a tidy up, he could easily find someone to move in. Even as early as the new year." She took a sip of her drink. "I just wish we knew someone who'd step in to help." She turned her gaze on me. "You know? Make the trip north for us? So we don't have to leave the property just sitting there." She fluttered her eyelashes. "Someone Harry and I can trust."

CHAPTER 2

"Oh no," I replied. Shaking my head, I let out a near hysterical laugh.

"Please, Antonia, you'd be helping us out no end."

Me, stuck in the middle of nowhere? My friend had to be joking. "But I hate the countryside. The countryside's full of cows and sheep. As for all that snow you just talked about, Jules..." I pictured myself slipping and sliding around in the stuff, desperate to stay upright. "Do you want me to end up like you? With a broken leg?"

Jules giggled, no doubt visualising the same thing.

"Then there are all those nosey neighbours," I carried on. "You know what villages are like. Everyone prying into everyone else's business." I shuddered, knowing I stood a better chance with the weather. "You're asking the wrong one here."

Jules's shoulders slumped. "Look, I understand you've never been a people person, but you'd be doing us a big favour."

I scoffed, unable to believe what I was hearing. "Jules, I live in London. I'm surrounded by people."

"Ah, but here no one wants to stop and chat, do they? Which

is just the way you like it. Londoners are too busy getting on with their own day to care about what's happening in yours."

I saw myself travelling on the Underground, aware that commuters would rather focus on their phones or read books than acknowledge their fellow passengers. Staring at their feet was preferable to saying hello. Moreover, in my experience, city dwellers wouldn't borrow a cup of sugar if their life depended on it. It'd be hypoglycaemia here we come! I frowned, and, forced to admit I included myself in that, realised Jules could be right.

"You never know, you might just find you love it up there," Jules continued, taking her positive thinking to a whole new level.

"Really?" I stared at my friend, deadpan.

"Please, Antonia." She gave me her best puppy-eyed plea. "You'll only be gone for a week."

I continued to look at her.

"Maybe two."

We both knew she was talking rubbish.

"Like Christmas is an issue for you anyway," Jules said, with no choice but to concede. "You're not exactly a fan of this time of year. I mean, how many offers have you had to come and spend the day here?" she asked. "And how many times have you turned us down?"

"It's not that I don't want to spend Christmas Day with you, I just don't go in for all that..."

Jules laughed. "Pomp and ceremony?"

I didn't like to say, but, yes, Jules and Harry did tend to go over the top. It was all posh frocks, expensive food, and extravagant gifts.

"Well if you can't put on a good show at Christmas, Mrs Ebenezer Scrooge, then when can you? Besides, that's what Christmas is all about. Surrounding yourself with people you love. Enjoying their company." She gave me a pointed look. "Spoiling them."

I couldn't deny Jules was right. The whole festive shebang had never been my thing. People might talk about "family" and "community spirit", but in my experience, what was in their stocking and having a good time seemed to take priority. So while everyone else was out partying or stressing over what was really an upmarket Sunday dinner, I shut my door, locked myself away, and watched Hallmark movies until New Year, only to reappear when the madness had begun to dissipate.

"And it's not as if you have anything else on at the moment, is it?"

Raising my cup to take a mouthful of coffee, I paused before it reached my lips. "Whose fault is that?" I asked. Putting on my sternest of voices, my eyes went from Jules to Frank.

There was no refuting I had a lot of time on my hands. Since my dog walking client list had dried up, finding another source of income had proved difficult. It seemed my chosen profession was tighter knit than I'd realised, and my unblemished record counted for nothing once word got out that prize-winning Delilah the Dachshund had fallen pregnant under my watch. The reputation I'd spent years building was shot. Owners the length and breadth of London no longer let me anywhere near their precious pooches. Apart from Jules, whose Heinz 57, Frank the mongrel, turned out to be none other than Delilah's baby-daddy.

Frank lifted his head, a whimper escaping his mouth as he looked my way. And while I gave him the steely eye, letting him know I hadn't quite forgotten his misdemeanour, it was clear he still hadn't forgiven me in return. It was after his dalliance with Delilah, that Jules and Harry had finally got round to getting him neutered.

"See it the same way as me. As a holiday," Jules said.

I rolled my eyes. My protests didn't seem to matter; the woman wasn't for giving up. But whereas working through a dead woman's possessions might be my friend's idea of a break, it certainly wasn't mine.

"In fact, forget sorting the house out. Let's face it, just to have someone get the place warmed up at this time of year's a bonus. Use Number 3 to relax. Stay for Christmas. It'll do you good to have some time out. To reassess and think about your future."

"My future?" Again, I wondered what the woman was talking about.

"Well, your savings aren't going to last forever, are they?"

I frowned at the thought of my depleting bank balance.

"You'll have to think about a new direction at some point. So why not now? You could even let Frank tag along." As the dog lifted his head again, his eyes suddenly full of optimism, Jules let out an exaggerated sigh. She looked down at her leg. "I can't even get to his bowl to feed him, let alone take him out to the park."

Taking in Frank's hopeful expression, my gaze went from him to Jules and back again. With the two of them suddenly working in tandem, I didn't just feel guilty, I felt myself sway. I pictured Frank enjoying the kind of freedom he didn't get in London, smiling to myself as wintry sun shone down on his wiry-haired back. His oversized ears lolloped around in all directions, smacking him in the face as he bounded through open field after open field. I could even hear Shakin' Stevens's "Merry Christmas Everyone" playing in the background.

My smile froze as hard as the snowy ground in my imagination. Acknowledging that Frank had a less than perfect recall, I realised I'd be the one chasing after him.

CHAPTER 3

Two weeks to Christmas

*V*iolet's engine coughed and spluttered. "Nearly there," I said, trying to sound cheery as I checked the satnav. Continuing to slip and slide on the icy road, I didn't know who I was trying to reassure the most – Frank, my trusty, yet nervous-looking, travel companion; or myself.

A thick blanket of cloud threatened more snow, and I gave Violet's steering wheel a comforting pat, encouraging her to keep going until we reached our destination. I knew when I bought the old Transit, I was taking a chance. But with money tight it made sense to spend as little as I could on my new venture, something I was beginning to regret. "How did I let you talk me into this?" I said, thinking of Jules.

Knowing exactly how, I giggled as I recalled my friend's face when I told her about my new business.

"You're going to be a skip rat?" she'd said, her expression a mix of confusion and horror.

"Roadside reclamation specialist, if you don't mind." I delved into my handbag, pulled out one of my hot-off-the-press business cards and handed it over. "See."

Not that my professional approach seemed to make any difference; Jules continued to appear less than impressed. "I don't think I've heard anything more ridiculous," she said.

"Have you any idea how many people are renovating property these days?" I asked. "I could make a fortune in London alone. Everyone's on the lookout for that one statement piece." My excitement built just thinking about it. "Well, I can get it for them." I snatched my business card back. "For a price."

"You are aware that what you're planning is illegal, right?" Jules said.

"Not if I ask permission before taking, it isn't." I wore a smug smile as I pointed to Jules's primary source of entertainment of late – the television. "And as you know, upcycling isn't just all the rage right now, it's profitable."

Jules chuckled. "Doesn't change anything though. You'll still be a skip rat." She laughed some more. "I can't wait to tell Harry."

I wouldn't have cared but it was her who had put the idea into my head.

"You can't go yet. You have to see this," Jules had said, the day she suggested I make the trip to Little Leatherington on her behalf. "It's a show about a woman who spends her days at the tip intercepting people's rubbish before they can throw it away."

"And why would she do that?" I asked.

"She repurposes stuff to sell on. Turns old ladders into pot racks and pianos into sideboards. That kind of thing."

"People throw away pianos?" I plonked myself back down on the sofa, my interest piqued.

"We're not talking about a Steinway Alma-Tadema. But with

a bit of creativity, some things become more valuable," Jules said. "That's how she earns her money."

By the end of the show, I'd seen the light.

Not long after that, it seemed so had Jules and firing up my imagination, on and on she went, talking about all the fantastic stock I'd be able to source up in the Yorkshire Dales. Proper authentic pieces, that were new to the London market. I needed somewhere to stay while carrying out such business dealings, of course, and it just so happened her Aunt Lillian's cottage would make the ideal base.

I shook my head at the recollection. Never mind Jules's job as a medical secretary, she would have made a fantastic saleswoman. Thanks to her patter, before I knew it, I'd bought a van, packed my bags, and hit the road. Talk about persuasive.

Frank shifted in the passenger seat and bringing my thoughts back to the present, I looked up to the heavens, cursing the second I'd agreed to Christmas in Little Leatherington. I'd known it would be cold, but while Jules had encouraged my new venture, backed up with stories of log fires, mulled wine, and roasting chestnuts, not once had she warned me about such freezing temperatures or the prospect of Violet breaking down smack bang in the middle of some wilderness.

While the drive had started off well enough, conditions had become increasingly difficult the further north we got. The sky went from having flashes of blue to a ceiling of grey. Rain showers came in, only to be replaced by hail and sleet, and, as the roads ascended to higher ground, eventually snow. Glancing around, I didn't think I'd seen a place so dismal.

Rugged drystone walls created a patchwork of white fields, while sheep, looking miserable and sodden, munched on frozen pasture. I'd never understood why people found living in the countryside romantic. From what I could see, the environment looked harsh and unforgiving. Not that I imagined it being any better in summer. In my view, once you'd seen one hill, you'd seen them all.

Much preferring the city landscape I'd left behind over the desolateness I found myself in, I pictured London's row upon row of houses, its packed cafés, thriving businesses, and chock-full restaurants. I saw brightly coloured Christmas lights heralding the way down Oxford and Regent streets, and crowds of people congregating to admire Harrods' Yuletide window display with shoppers weaving from one store to the next as they frantically hunted and gathered for the upcoming festivities. And while all the Christmas fanfare might not have been my thing, I couldn't deny it beat driving around in the middle of nowhere.

A big stone farmhouse ahead caught my attention, the first property I'd seen in miles. My eyes lit up and my spirits lifted. It appeared Christmas had come early and feeling guilty for all the moaning, I told myself I should have known my friend's instincts would be right. As I took in the big yellow skip in the house's front garden, London's busy streets paled in significance. I felt excited yet nervous at the prospect of making my first acquisition. "What do you think, Frank?" I said. "Shall we do this?"

I'd never knocked on a stranger's door to ask if I could liberate their rubbish before and wondering how my request would be received, I brought Violet to a standstill. Leaving her engine running for fear of it not starting again, I took off my seat belt, steeling myself ready to find out.

Frank bolted upright. Putting his front paws on the passenger door armrest and his nose to the window, he wagged his tail at the prospect of freedom.

"Sorry, boy," I said. "Not this time."

He whined in what sounded like protest, but I remained steadfast and while he sat sulking, I turned my attention back to the skip. Pleased to spot an old wooden chair poking out of the top, even from a distance I could see it was made from pine, and not that rubbish orange stuff either. Clapping my hands together, I couldn't wait to find out what other delights lay in store.

Getting ready to disembark, I caught my reflection in the rear-view mirror. My hair hung down from under my bobble hat, and seeing it looked raggedy, I hastily smoothed it straight. Wearing a thick padded jacket and jeans, I wished I looked a tad more professional. But I reached into the passenger footwell and dug out a business card from my rucksack then put on my best smile, determined to create a good impression. "I won't be a minute," I said to Frank, eager to get my hands on anything that might turn a profit.

As soon as I climbed out of the van, the ice-cold air immediately hit me. I couldn't believe how glacial the atmosphere felt and I shivered as my breath steamed forth. After hours of driving my back ached and I began to stretch it out, but suddenly my feet slid from under me and my stomach lurched, as I grabbed the side of the van to right myself before I could hit the ground. Praying no one had borne witness, I took a step forward and keeping my eyes down as I walked to stop me slipping again, I made sure to concentrate as I headed towards the house's entrance. If I wasn't careful, I'd be spending Christmas in the same predicament as Jules – wearing a cast.

With no sign of a doorbell, I picked up the heavy brass knocker and rapped as hard as I could. I refused to let my excitement wane as I stamped my feet and breathed into my hands to keep warm. I knocked again, before leaning back slightly to get a glimpse through the window. With no sign of movement my shoulders slumped and my smile fell. It seemed I wasn't about to bag my first find, after all, and with no choice but to concede, I turned and headed back to Violet.

Passing the skip again, I stopped in my tracks and unable to help myself, took a moment to inspect the chair. I reached up and ran my gloved fingers up and down its well-worn wood and despite there being no sign of woodworm, I could tell it was old. Already imagining it cleaned up and sitting pride of place next to a fashionable Aga in some posh London kitchen, I felt a frisson of naughtiness, aware that if I wanted to, I could just grab the chair and throw it into the van. After all, it was headed for the tip; it wasn't as if anyone would miss it. I looked left and then right, my mischievous side knowing that with no one around, the odds of getting away with it were in my favour.

CHAPTER 4

As I got back into the van and pulled out onto the open road, I pushed away my disappointment over the chair. But no way was I breaking the law over a simple piece of furniture. Whacking up the heater to warm myself after being out in the cold, I resolved to return another day.

I had plenty of time to scout the area for stock. Unlike most people it wasn't as if I had a busy Christmas ahead of me. As usual, I had no friends or family about to descend and no big day to get ready for, leaving me with ample opportunity to focus on my new venture, interruption free. Even if I didn't see another yellow skip again during my stay, I still had lots to be getting on with. I envisaged ticking off items on my long to-do list. Sorting out a website, setting up relevant social media accounts, coming up with a fabulous name for my business and locating suitable storage and workshop space. My flat in London was way too small to house other people's discarded furniture, and even if I did try to squeeze a couple of bits in, I doubted my landlord would approve.

The road suddenly veered to the left and I was forced to drop the van a gear. Violet juddered in protest as we approached a little hamlet consisting of a handful of houses. It was like driving through a scene on a Christmas card. Smoke billowed from chimneys and a golden glow shone out through mullion windows, while the covering of snow completed the picture. Had she been able to make the journey, Jules would have loved it. I thought about all the activities my friend had had planned for her and Harry. A magical winter woodland stroll, a ride on a steam train, partaking in a Dickensian Christmas experience... All very in keeping with the environment around me. And romantic, I supposed. Not that there was any point in me thinking that way.

Two women, wrapped up in thick coats and woolly scarves, stood at one of the garden gates chatting and while I gripped Violet's steering wheel so as not to lose control on the ice, the van jolted and backfired, abruptly interrupting them mid-sentence. They stared into my vehicle as I advanced, clearly intent on getting a good look at me.

Typical village nosiness, I realised, frowning at the attention. I readily imagined them getting straight on the phone to Little Leatherington, announcing the fact that a stranger was on her way into the village. An unnecessary exercise, in my view. As the van let out another loud bang, followed by a thick plume of exhaust smoke, it was clear the racket Violet made was warning enough.

Levelling out onto a straight, I left the gossiping duo behind. Staring ahead, the road appeared never-ending and with nothing but stretches of fields to my left and right as far as the eye could see, it seemed Little Leatherington was more remote than I'd anticipated. I sighed. Having hoped to have a bit of time to myself, I had to wonder what I was supposed to do for leisure. Frank might have loved running around in the great outdoors for hours on end, but that wasn't my idea of fun. Scott of the Antarctic I was not.

Sporadic patches of grass had started to poke through the white. "At least the snow's beginning to clear, eh, Frank," I said. A welcome indication that finally, we were descending from higher ground.

I spotted a *Welcome to Little Leatherington* sign and as the road bore left, I felt my spirits lift. "Look, Frank," I said, hoping the sight before me wasn't a desperation-induced mirage. "It's a pub." A traditional white rendered building, The Cobblestone Tavern had wooden sash windows and olde worlde signage and as with every other chimney I'd seen, smoke caught in the wind as it rose out of its stack. Less enamouring was the giant inflatable Santa Claus strapped to the establishment's roof. It swung and swayed in the wind, like something from a low budget festive-themed horror movie.

Dismissing the blow-up Santa altogether, I looked forward to sitting by the pub's open fire, with my head in a book, and Frank by my feet. "That's our evening sorted," I said. After the long drive up, I couldn't think of anything better than a glass of something nice. "And there's a shop," I said, as we continued on our way. Just knowing I wouldn't have to drive miles if we ran out of milk made me, once again, feel like Christmas had come early.

The chequered flag appeared on the satnav and I slowed Violet to a standstill. She choked and gasped as we pulled up outside Aunt Lillian's terraced cottage. The van was obviously as glad as I was to reach our destination; like me, she seemed to sigh as I switched off her engine. "Here at last," I said, to Frank, who was already on his feet, tail wagging and nose to the window.

Turning my attention to what was to be my home for the next few weeks, my heart immediately sank. I whimpered at the sight. Number 3, Bluebell Row, wasn't anything like the quaint little abode that Jules had talked about. Unlike Frank, who seemed keen to see more, I wasn't sure if I dared go in.

Jules had described her aunt as a proud woman who plumed at having the nicest home on the street and not just on the inside. Apparently, thanks to the woman's green fingers, both the front and back gardens bloomed all year round. Her skill at nurturing even the weakest of plants was the envy of the village.

"Not anymore," I said. I took in the cottage's tired, flaking paintwork, the dead brown plants that were no longer recognisable, and the leaning, weathered garden gate. I glanced at the neighbouring houses, with their manicured designs, evergreen hedges, and welcoming Christmas lights. Aunt Lillian's house now stood out for all the wrong reasons.

I reminded myself that not only had it been years since Jules's last visit, the old lady had been well into her nineties when she'd passed. In Aunt Lillian's later years, making sure she didn't break a hip would've been more of a priority than DIY and gardening. Still, if the outside was anything to go by, the property required more than the *bit of a tidy up* that Jules had mentioned. Getting the place ready for any potential tenant would take graft and I could already see my friend's disappointment when she received the photos I'd promised to take, especially when she'd hoped for a quick turnaround.

The front door opened and as a gentleman appeared I smiled, immediately deciding to focus on the positives. "A pub, a shop, and a handsome chap, Frank." I smoothed down my hair. "They say all good things come in threes." While Jules had told me the letting agent would be on hand when I landed to show me around, she'd failed to say how good-looking the man was. "Oliver Chase, I presume."

CHAPTER 5

*J*eans, a white shirt, and a fine knit V-neck sweater: Oliver Chase's attire couldn't have contrasted more with the suited and booted dress code of London-based property managers. Oliver Chase wore no tie and he had heavy-soled, tan boots on his feet, instead of shiny black lace-ups. Taking in his swept-back blond hair and welcoming smile, such a casual appearance only added to the man's physical appeal. I smiled back at him, trying to create a good impression. Not only was the man attractive, working in property, he'd know where all the best skips were.

As the letting agent made his approach, Frank jumped up and down at the passenger window, wagging his tail at the possibility of making a new friend. "You can't get out yet," I said to the dog, thinking it would be better to get business out of the way before letting him loose on anyone.

Frank looked at me through the most pitiful eyes and I immediately felt guilty.

"Oh, all right," I said, grabbing my rucksack and clipping his lead to his collar. "You win."

Frank scrambled to meet Oliver as we got out of the van. I

kept the lead tight to prevent him from getting too out of control and, throwing my rucksack over my shoulder, tried to appear cool and collected. "Mr Chase," I said, almost tripping. With one arm outstretched ready to formally introduce myself, Frank continuing to tug at the other, and a layer of ice beneath my feet, it was all I could do to stay upright.

"Please," he replied. "Call me Oliver." Even more handsome up close, the man held my gaze as he shook my hand. He had striking green eyes and his grip was firm yet controlled.

"Antonia," I said, transfixed.

He raised an eyebrow as I continued to hold his hand, an action that brought me back to my senses and I quickly let go.

"*Sei Italiana?*" he said.

It was obvious Oliver was asking if I was Italian and although, unlike him, I couldn't speak a word of the language, I felt tempted to pretend I at least had Roman roots. I knew I'd get away with it thanks to my long dark hair, but in the end I couldn't lie, not even to impress. I shook my head. "A mother with a thing for Antonio Banderas."

"Really?" Oliver bit down on his lips, clearly trying not to laugh.

I didn't mind his amusement. I was used to it. "She was what you'd call a superfan. I'm named after him."

"Was?"

"Mum's no longer with us."

A look of understanding crossed Oliver's face. "I'm sorry to hear that." He turned his attention to my four-legged friend, crouching down to tickle the dog's overly long ears. "And who's this?"

"Frank," I replied, rolling my eyes as despite the freezing ground the dog threw himself down on his back for a belly rub.

"What a handsome fellow," Oliver said, happily doing Frank's bidding.

Handsome was not a word I'd have used.

I thought back to when Jules and Harry first introduced me to Frank. He had to be the cutest puppy on the planet with his big brown eyes, sleek black fur, and the best of temperaments. Little did anyone know that while he'd keep his friendly nature, his looks wouldn't fare quite so well. Rather, he'd turn into a stumpy, wiry-furred lump that was so ugly, he'd end up with a face only I, Jules, and Harry could love.

"It's all Collies and gun dogs around here," Oliver said. "And none of them as good looking as you, eh, boy?"

I smiled at his words. Attractive and non-judgemental on the animal front; I was impressed. As was Frank, I noted. Belly up, legs wide and tongue hanging out, the dog relished the attention.

Rising to his feet, Oliver looked from me to Violet. "Good drive up?" he asked.

"Yes, thank you." At last, Frank stood up too. He sniffed the ground around our feet, before cocking his leg at the gatepost to have what had to be the longest wee known to man. "Although I have to say I'm glad it's over with," I said, pretending not to notice.

"Looks like you're not the only one," Oliver said, doing no such thing. Instead, he nodded at Frank, who without a care in the world continued to empty his bladder.

I glared at the dog, wondering how he could embarrass me like that.

"Now to business," Oliver said. "I suppose I should start by welcoming you to Little Leatherington. You've picked a great time of year to come visit." He gestured to the hills. "You can't get more Christmassy than this."

I followed his gaze. "Oxford Street might beg to differ," I said.

Oliver looked at me as if confused.

"The trouble they go to with their window displays."

At last his face broke into a smile. "You almost had me there," he said, looking at me direct. "I like a woman with a sense of humour." He drew my attention to Aunt Lillian's cottage. "As you can see, the house needs a bit of work."

"And I like a man with optimism," I said. We were obviously seeing two different things.

Oliver let out a laugh. "Honestly. It's not as bad as it seems. To be fair to Lillian, she took great care of the place."

"You knew her?"

"Everyone knew Lillian. She was quite a lady. The stories that woman could tell. The village isn't the same without her."

I recalled Jules telling me what a character her aunt could be. Unusual for a woman of her generation, Lillian never married. She had no desire to have children so didn't see the point and, despite several proposals over the years, she much preferred the freedom that came with her single status. Apparently, she caught the travelling bug at a young age and according to my friend there wasn't a continent that Lillian hadn't visited. "Jules was saddened when she couldn't make the funeral," I said. "They might not have seen each other for some time, but she remembers her aunt fondly."

"Knowing Lillian, she wouldn't have minded," Oliver said. "She wasn't one for ceremonial duties."

The more I heard about Jules's Aunt Lillian, the more I liked her.

Oliver got back to business, once again focusing on Number 3, Bluebell Row. "You might not think so to look at them, but the windows are actually quite solid, and the garden just needs a tidy up."

"And inside?" I said, tentative.

"I thought you'd never ask," Oliver said. "If we stand here much longer, I'll freeze." He grinned as he gestured to the front door. "After you."

CHAPTER 6

$\mathcal{A}$ s I stepped over the threshold, my eyes widened in delight at the sight that greeted me. I felt like I'd been transported back to the Victorian era. The hallway's beige carpet might not have been in keeping with that period, but the walls were papered in a beautiful vintage floral damask, and designed in burgundies, coppers and greens, which had a gold shimmer to it. A solid wood staircase led up to the bedrooms. Clearly original, not only could I see where its banister had been worn by hands sweeping up and down over the years, it still had its ball-shaped finials, top and bottom.

The decor might not have been quite to my taste, but I couldn't deny how fabulous it was and I had to admit the house felt warm and welcoming.

I let Frank off his lead so he could go and explore, while Oliver leaned down and tugged at the corner of the flooring. "I've already had a peek," he said, pulling back the carpet to reveal the most beautiful black, beige and terracotta tiles. "What do you think?"

Keen to give them a closer inspection, I lowered myself down to his level, suddenly caught off guard by a waft of the man's aftershave. I took a deep breath, savouring the fragrance. Oliver Chase smelt as divine as he looked.

He turned his head to look at me and with his face inches from mine I did my best not to blush.

"Hopefully, there'll be more secrets to uncover," he said.

His words woke me from my scent-induced trance. "Excuse me?" Convinced I must have misheard, I stared at Oliver, aghast. Nobody had said anything to me about redecorating or restoring. In fact, Jules had distinctly told me not to do anything. Oliver laughed as he rose to his feet, ready to continue with the tour, while I made a mental note to contact my friend and clarify exactly what my remit was.

"Don't worry. I'm under strict instructions not to let you do anything to the house. Everything has to stay exactly as it is. I just thought you could let Jules know it's not all doom and gloom. The house does have its good points."

He indicated a room off to the right and following him in, my eyes were immediately drawn to the cast-iron fireplace with flames dancing in the hearth. I took off my hat, gloves, and jacket; after being out in the cold the warmth was just what I needed.

"I thought you might appreciate me setting the fire in readiness," Oliver said.

"I do," I replied. "Definitely." The man was an angel.

I glanced around. Pictures and framed photos filled the walls, while a floral three-piece suite took up the centre of the room. I noticed that Oliver's coat lay slung over the back of the sofa. The seating was clearly arranged to make the most of the fire, in front of which sat a rug, while the rest of the floor had been left boarded. Against one wall was a display cabinet, crammed with ornaments, while a solid dark wood sideboard sat against another. I dreaded to think how much stuff the latter piece contained but going off the clutter on top of it, I could hazard a guess. I filled my cheeks with air and slowly exhaled.

For all anyone knew, Jules's Aunt Lillian could have been born at Number 3, Bluebell Row – which meant I could've been surrounded by almost a hundred years of personal possessions.

"It would seem Lillian was a bit of a collector," Oliver said, as if reading my mind.

"It certainly looks that way," I replied. But at least the place was clean, I had to acknowledge.

Frank appeared in the doorway, took one look around and then left again.

I chuckled. "He's got the right idea," I said, relieved it wasn't my job to sort everything out.

"I can give you the names of a couple of valuers to pass on if you like?" Oliver said. "To scan their expert eyes over everything. When Jules is ready, of course?"

"She'd appreciate that." I moved to take a closer look at one of Lillian's photos. Black and white, it was of a glamorous young woman. She wore a button-down shirt, tucked into high-waisted, wide-legged swing pants and her shoes were two-tone loafers. The whole ensemble looked wonderful. "Is that Lillian?" I asked.

Oliver came for a closer look. "It certainly is."

"She clearly had a strong sense of style as well as adventure," I said. I looked down at my oversized woolly sweater, scruffy jeans and Doc Martens boots, feeling positively dowdy in comparison.

Oliver grinned, but before he could say anything his phone began to ring. Pulling it out of his jeans pocket, he checked the number. "Mind if I take this?" he said, before clicking the answer button.

I left him to his call and made my way out and down the hall to the kitchen. Like the rest of what I'd seen, the room was spotless yet dated. Consisting of wooden units, an old ceramic sink, and an electric cooker, it didn't have the same romanticism as the hallway and living room. But it had the basics like a washing machine, a dining table, and a couple of chairs. The walls were pasted with paper designed to look like tiling. It was all right for me, who was staying rent-free, but I couldn't imagine a paying tenant being very happy with it.

I looked out of the window onto the rear garden, to see a long winding path cut down the middle of a dead lawn, leading to what looked like a stone workshop at the end. Flowerless borders followed the fence line on both sides, and the stems that were out there were brown and brittle. There was a definite order to the space, and I could imagine how beautiful it would have been when Lillian was at her green-fingered best and it was filled with colour.

"Sorry about that," Oliver said, interrupting my reverie as he appeared in the kitchen doorway, coat in hand. "A plumbing emergency in the next village."

"The life of a letting agent, eh," I said.

"Frozen pipes. Happens every winter," he replied. "I'm afraid I'm going to have to leave you to it." He dipped his hand into his jeans pocket and pulled out a business card, handing it over along with Aunt Lillian's house keys. "My contact numbers. Office and mobile."

"Thank you," I said.

"I'm only up the road, so if you need anything, please, just give me a shout."

"Anything?" I asked, wondering what services the man had to offer that didn't involve property. My cheeks flushed red and wanting the ground to open up and swallow me whole, I couldn't believe I'd just said that out loud.

"Within reason," he replied, making me blush even more.

"I'll see you to the door, shall I?" I said.

CHAPTER 7

*H*aving brought all my stuff in from the van, explored the whole house and taken a ridiculous number of photos to send to Jules, I headed back into the lounge, Frank following. I didn't envy Jules when it came to sorting the place out. Having seen everything first-hand, I felt daunted on my friend's behalf. I wouldn't have known where to start.

The whole property was a treasure trove of the weird and the wonderful. Jules hadn't been exaggerating when she said her aunt liked to travel. The place was filled with interesting keepsakes and souvenirs from countries near and far. The furniture was gorgeous, and I would have put money on most of it being antique. Even inside the woman's wardrobe was a sight to behold. When it came to what she wore, Lillian did like high-end. Jules should certainly get good use out of Oliver's list of valuers.

I plonked myself down on the sofa and with a whole evening ahead, checked my watch. "We could watch a bit of telly?" I said to Frank, deciding it was a bit early to go for that deserved glass of wine. Although being honest, I wasn't really in the mood for TV. I glanced around, twiddling my thumbs as I questioned what was wrong with me. I usually loved my own company but sitting there in the silence, in a strange house, even reading one of the books I'd brought, didn't appeal. Maybe the drive up had got to me? For someone not used to negotiating snow and ice, it had taken quite a lot of concentration. Or it could have been the fact that I was surrounded by Lillian's possessions. They made her feel very much present and me very much the interloper.

I sighed. "Sod it," I said, thinking it was time for that drink, after all. "What do you say, Frank? Fancy getting out of here?" I smiled as the dog's tail began to wag. "Of course you do."

I grabbed my rucksack off the sofa, stuffed Lillian's house keys into one of its side pockets and grabbed Frank's lead. Clipping it onto his collar, I put on my coat and buttoned it up tight, steeling myself for the cold air about to greet us. As we made our way outside into the fading light, I took a deep breath, ready to meet the locals.

Frank kept his nose down as we walked. With lots of new smells to investigate, he'd obviously hit upon an invisible trail, and while he followed his nose, I took in the rest of our surroundings.

Little Leatherington consisted of a single road straight through the village, in one end and out at the other. It was lined with both terraced and detached cottages and Christmas trees with twinkling fairy lights sat in windows and holly wreaths adorned front doors. Farmhouses dotted the hillside beyond and a glorious full moon lit up the giant, snow-capped mountain that stood proud in the distance. Taking in the trail that snaked up to its summit, I wondered who'd be mad enough to make such a trek. In my view, there was too much danger to even consider trying – mud deep enough to sink into, stiles befitting of any good obstacle course, not to mention charging sheep. "We'll be all right if we stick to the roads, Frank," I said. No way were we venturing up there.

A car coming towards us caught my attention and I couldn't help but smile at the sight. It looked like something straight off the set of *All Creatures Great and Small*. British racing green in colour, its roof was black and could be folded back, and it had a silver grill taller than any I'd seen before. I didn't have a clue what make the car was, but it had to be from the 1930s and it was certainly at home amongst all the old stone cottages and surrounding farmland. No way would it have been out and about in London at that time of year; it would have been garaged, only hitting the roads on the driest and sunniest of days.

Its driver, a middle-aged, tweed-wearing somewhat smart gentleman, smiled and waved before giving two sharp toots on the car horn as he passed. I waved back, before shaking my head as Frank and I, too, carried on our way. It seemed Lillian wasn't the only character to come out of Little Leatherington.

Continuing straight past the shop, I saw the pub's giant rooftop Santa before I saw The Cobblestone Tavern itself and watching the inflatable bounce around in the wind, I didn't think I'd seen anything so ludicrous. Or so out of keeping, I realised, considering how traditional the rest of the village was. Pulling open the door and crossing over the threshold into the porch, I noticed a poster advertising a Christmas party being held there. I frowned, recalling the aftermath of such events as heard from the safety of my London home over the years. Forced to endure various renditions of festive tunes by passing partygoers down in the street, from George Michael's "Last Christmas" to the Pogues' "Fairytale of New York", I couldn't imagine anything worse than seeing such drunken shenanigans first-hand.

As I stepped into the bar, however, I immediately froze and

all thoughts of blow-up Santas and badly sung Christmas number ones suddenly evaporated. Even a place as small and remote as Little Leatherington wasn't free from all the excesses of Christmas and my eyes widened at the nightmare I seemed to have walked into. Glancing from one corner of the room, to the next, and then the next, I stood there, horrified, forced to take in shelf after shelf of ornamental Santas. Some carried sacks, while others hung halfway up miniature ladders. Some rode on sleighs and some had their heads popping out of chimneys. Unlike all the other customers, who didn't appear to notice the hundreds of Santa eyes looking down on them, I wanted to turn around and run.

"What can I get you?" the barwoman called out before I got the chance.

As well as a big smile, she wore a bright red jumper with a huge snowman plastered across the front, while dangly Christmas tree earrings that flashed red and gold hung from the woman's ears; both enough to tell me she was responsible for the Father Christmas overload. "Sauvignon Blanc, please," I said. If I'd thought I'd needed a drink before, it was nothing to how I felt then.

"Large or small?"

"Large," I replied, a bit too quickly. My belly began to rumble, reminding me that I hadn't yet had dinner. "Do you have a menu?" I asked, deciding I may as well eat there too.

"We do."

I glanced around again, this time in search of a seat. There was a huge wood burner to one side of the room, but the place was packed, and I struggled to spot *any* seat, let alone one by the fire.

"Darts night," the barwoman said. She indicated a room at the other side of the bar just as a euphoric cheer sounded. "Last match before Christmas."

Appreciating the explanation, my heart sank when I realised the only place available meant sharing a table with an elderly bearded gentleman. A chap who wore a scowl so serious it could have turned my wine sour.

The barwoman gave me a sympathetic smile and despite my feet not wanting to move, I took a deep breath. Carrying my glass and the menu in one hand, while pulling Frank along with the other, I made my approach. "Do you mind if I join you?" I asked, indicating the empty seat.

The man looked back at me, his stern expression unwavering. "And if I say yes, I do mind?"

My smile disappeared along with my politeness. "Then you'll have a decision to make, won't you?" I replied. Sitting down, I nodded to the exit. "The door's there if you want it."

The man harrumphed in response, while I wondered what his problem was.

Frank lay down next to my feet and I took a sip of my drink, before turning my attention to the menu. Refusing to meet his gaze, I felt the old man's eyes on me as I attempted to read. All I'd wanted was a quiet drink and maybe something to eat, but this chap seemed to be challenging me to a staring competition. However, I had no intention of taking part and kept my eyes down, all the while wishing I'd stayed stood at the bar. Or better still, stayed at Number 3. I sighed. Or even better, stayed in London.

"You tried to steal my chair," the man said.

I paused in my thoughts, before letting the menu drop to focus on the man and his allegation. I wondered if he suffered from age-related senility because I had just asked if I could sit down.

"I saw you. Earlier today."

Narrowing my eyes, I recalled my pit stop at the farmhouse with the skip in its front garden. Realising the man was talking about the pine chair, I was surprised to hear there'd been someone at home, after all. "If you saw me," I replied, curious to know where he was going with his conversation, "then you know full well I did nothing of the sort."

"You wanted to, though."

Admittedly, I'd been tempted, but that didn't stop me wondering who the man before me thought he was. A member of the mind police? "Furthermore," I said, "if you saw me, you must also have heard me knock."

The man picked up his pint, put it to his lips and drank until his glass was empty. "No law against not answering the door," he finally said.

"I agree. But there is a law against making things up about people. I could sue you for slander."

The man rose to his feet and without saying another word headed for the door, leaving me sat there open-mouthed.

Watching him go, I couldn't believe the man's rudeness and I told myself he could blooming well keep his chair. I shook my head at his accusation, shocked that someone would make up such a thing. "Well, that was weird," I said to Frank.

The barwoman approached to collect the old man's discarded glass. "I wouldn't take it personally," she said. "Ted Sharples is Little Leatherington's oldest and grumpiest resident. It's just his way. He's miserable with everyone."

CHAPTER 8

Still in my pyjamas, I made my way downstairs and into the kitchen. I felt refreshed and ready for the day ahead, having slept surprisingly well considering I was in a strange house, in a strange village, made up of strange people. A hot bath, clean fresh bedding, and a village with very few street lights was just the tonic I'd needed. I couldn't remember the last time I'd had such a good rest.

I recalled the previous night when I'd climbed into bed. Switching off the lamp, it was as if I'd suddenly lost my sight. I'd never known darkness like it. Lying there in the pitch black was a strange experience; it felt daunting. And the quiet. There were no car engines, no drunken mayhem, and no clattering of shutters as late-night businesses closed. The only sound had been Frank's rhythmic snoring. It was no wonder I'd enjoyed hours of unbroken blissful sleep.

Having organised myself the previous evening, I'd already set aside a notepad and pen and charged up my laptop in preparation of a productive day ahead. Jobwise, whereas other people were winding down in anticipation of the upcoming festivities, I intended on stepping up a gear so that I could hit the ground running when I got back to London. It felt good to know that my break in Little Leatherington meant I could get on with things uninterrupted. My eyes went from my laptop to the kettle. "First things first, though," I said, assessing my priorities. "Coffee."

My phone bleeped indicating a text had come through. I didn't recognise the number. I opened the message and, feeling a frisson of excitement, I couldn't help but smile. With no communiqué to pass on to Jules about Number 3, Bluebell Row, it appeared Mr Oliver Chase just wanted to check on my welfare and reiterate he was around if I needed anything. As I placed the phone back down on the counter, I couldn't recall giving him my number. I realised Jules must have handed it over, which made sense. Oliver was the letting agent Jules had instructed, after all, and I was her contact on the ground.

My phone bleeped again and picking it up once more I was surprised to see Oliver had sent another text.

How about I show you the sights? Pick you and Frank up in half an hour. If you fancy it?

My heart skipped a beat. Handsome men weren't in the habit of offering to take me out. Wondering what kind of sights he had in mind, I let my mind wander and pictured us on a romantic steam train ride like the one Jules had mentioned. I could hear the guard's whistle as we climbed aboard and the locomotive's hissing steam as we set off, followed by the chugging of its wheels gathering momentum on the track.

I let out a wistful sigh, forcing myself back to reality. While it was nice to daydream, no matter how much fantasising I did, the man was only trying to impress my friend. He probably thought looking after me demonstrated how well he'd look after any future tenant.

Needless to say, it wasn't as if I was really interested in him either. I had too much to think about sorting out my life. Setting up a new business was hard enough; and getting to know any local would be one distraction too many. Let alone a local as gorgeous as Mr Oliver Chase.

I looked from the phone in my hand, to my laptop, and back again. Re-evaluating Oliver's offer, I reasoned it wouldn't hurt to get a feel for the place, seeing as I was there for the foreseeable, especially when for all I knew, we might come across a few skips on our travels. Plus, it meant I could give Jules a proper low-down on the area, I told myself. Agreeing to go was as much for her benefit as it was mine.

I checked the weather through the window and, pleased to see the sun shone, thought it perfect for a day of sightseeing. "What do you think, Frank?" I asked, already imagining me, Oliver and the dog sat outside a little street café, enjoying a mid-morning cinnamon latte and a deep-filled mince pie with a huge blob of thick brandy cream.

The dog barked and wagged his tail.

"I'll take that as a yes," I said, replying to Oliver's text telling him I'd be ready and waiting before I could change my mind.

I raced upstairs to get ready, but thanks to there being no dilemma over what to wear, it didn't take long to get showered and dressed. I hadn't brought much with me clothing-wise. Sitting behind a computer and walking Frank didn't call for anything special on the attire front, so it hadn't crossed my mind to pack anything more than jeans and sweaters. However, what I did have was clean and comfortable, and, in freezing temperatures, perfect for strolling around a market town or enjoying a casual lunch.

Hearing a knock at the door, I threw on my coat and clipped Frank's lead to his collar before answering.

"Ready?" Oliver asked.

Seeing him standing there in jeans, walking boots, and a thick waterproof jacket, I felt relieved that I hadn't brought anything snazzier to wear. Knowing me, I'd have put it on and there is nothing more embarrassing than being overdressed. "Ready and able," I said, in answer to Oliver's question.

While Frank jumped up and down in excitement, his lead tangled around his stumpy legs and as Oliver leant down to free him, I locked up the house behind us.

"Shall we?" Oliver said, gesturing down the street.

Following him, I wondered where he'd parked his car. But instead of directing us towards a vehicle, we turned down a lane and continued on foot.

"So how was your first night here?" Oliver asked.

"Wonderful," I replied, confused about where we were going. "I slept harder than I've ever slept in my life."

"So you're full of energy this morning?"

"To the brim," I replied, laughing.

The man was obviously starting his tour of the area in our immediate vicinity, I reasoned, and we continued to chat as we walked. I let Frank off his lead under strict instructions not to do a runner and the dog trotted ahead, while Oliver talked about his life in the Dales and I about mine in London.

"Very different to here then," Oliver said, comparing the calm around us to the city's hectic environment.

"The polar opposite," I replied.

"I'm not sure I could live in a place like London full time," Oliver said. "I'd struggle to switch off."

"Here, I'd struggle to switch on. I mean, it's all right for a visit, to recharge your batteries. But after a while... Don't you get bored?"

"Believe me, life here is anything but. Besides, Leeds is only a train ride away if the city beckons."

I stopped still. "Sounds like you're trying to sell this place to me?"

A twinkle appeared in Oliver's eyes as he, too, came to a halt. "Maybe I am," he said, before picking up his step again.

We approached a wooden bridge that took us over a river. I stopped at its halfway point to look at the water as it bubbled over rocks and a fallen tree branch.

"This is the River Ribble," Oliver said. "It starts not far from here." He pointed in some general direction. "And runs into the Irish sea at Lytham in Lancashire."

I tried to look interested, but when Oliver had offered to show me the sights, the confirmed city girl in me hadn't anticipated going on a nature trail. I'd expected to do all the things tourists do. Lots of pavement pounding, being introduced to architecture, and maybe taking in a gallery showing work by local artists. Glancing around, with nothing but fields and trees and a river around us, we seemed to be moving further and further away from civilisation. "Are we headed anywhere in particular?" I asked, hoping he'd tell me about a charming little tea room or pottery studio hidden away.

"We are," Oliver replied, which told me nothing.

The more progress we made, the hotter, more bothered, and more apprehensive I became. As we plodded along, the road underfoot got narrower and the wind stronger. Coming at us from behind, the gust seemed to push us onwards. And upwards, I noted.

I scanned the area again, wondering when this bit of my sightseeing tour would finish. My eyes hit on a pathway carved into the hillside just ahead and following its trail, I froze. "Oliver," I said, bringing myself to a standstill. "You're not planning on showing me the sights in one single hit, are you?"

Oliver paused in his step to look at me. He grinned.

My stomach lurched.

His smile said it all.

CHAPTER 9

*W*ith my cheek squashed against the icy rock face, I clung to the mountainside like a limpet as if my life depended on it. I didn't know who or what howled the loudest – me or the swirling winds that whipped around my already contorted face. As the gusts threatened to rip me from what little security I had, flying without wings was not how I'd imagined my final moments. "Tell Jules I'm sorry for ruining her Christmas," I said while I still had the chance, voice raised and mid-wail.

"I'm the one who's sorry, Antonia," Oliver said, calling up from the ledge below. "If I'd have known your legs weren't long enough…"

"I know, I know. Hindsight's a wonderful thing!"

"Are you sure you can't go any higher? There can't be much more than a metre left."

"If I could, don't you think I'd be up by now?" Peeling my cheek off the rock, I carefully glanced about me. Double-checking all the nearby indents and protruding rocks, it was no good. They were all out of my reach. I tilted my chin and looked down to see Oliver's concerned expression and Frank's head poking out of the man's rucksack. As tears rolled down my face, I couldn't believe Oliver had suggested I go first. The other way around and he could have shimmied up with Frank, then reached down and yanked me the rest of the way.

I also couldn't believe my foolishness. It might've only been a small section of our walk as far as Oliver was concerned, but he was used to it. He'd been going up and down Fotherghyll Fell since he was a child. I, on the other hand, was from London. In the city, if people wanted to enjoy the view, they rode on the London Eye or took a lift and dined in a high-rise restaurant. They didn't scale mountains. No wonder I was stuck.

"You're doing great," Oliver said.

Considering my predicament, it was going to take a lot more than platitudes to lift my spirits. Ice seeped through my gloves and my hands felt numb. My lips quivered uncontrollably, and as I continued to battle the wind, I felt so cold my legs began to shake. My heart raced. Not sure how much longer I could hold on, I was convinced I was about to fall to my death.

"Help will be here soon. I promise."

More tears rolled down my face. Mountain rescue... Like I hadn't lost enough dignity.

Forced to hang there for I didn't know how long, Oliver continued to try to reassure me, but with my energy levels dwindling, it was to no avail.

"Tell Jules I'll need a closed coffin," I said. No longer able to discern how tight my grip was, I wagered it wouldn't be too long until I fell.

"Please, Antonia," Oliver replied, his voice concerned. "That's no way to talk."

"What? You're going to catch me on my way down, are you?" Full of self-pity, I knew I sounded like a stroppy teenager, but I couldn't help myself.

"There won't be any need for that," a voice from above said.

My gaze shot up to see three men in bright red waterproofs and yellow safety helmets. Although as far as I was concerned, they weren't wearing helmets at all; they wore halos. They carried coils of orange rope, one of which they seemed to be pegging into the crag.

"Don't worry," Man Number Two said. "We'll soon have you down safe and sound."

I heard more voices coming from below and daring to look their way, I saw that two more red-clothed and yellow-hatted individuals had arrived. "I can't believe this is happening," I said, once again wishing I was anywhere but there. I closed my eyes and thanks to the shame of it all, felt tempted to just throw myself off the mountain to get it over with. At least then I wouldn't have to deal with any ridicule. "Ouch!" My eyes opened as something hit me on the head. Brought back to my senses, I squinted as I looked up to check I wasn't in harm's way.

"Just a loose chipping," the third of the upper trio said. Ready to start his descent, Man Number Three's colleagues paid out his rope through the lowering system they'd rigged, so he could gradually let himself down towards me. "Nothing to worry about."

"Easy for you to say!" I replied.

At last, he drew level. "Antonia?"

I nodded.

"So you're the woman I've been hearing all about."

"Sorry?"

"You can call me Barrowboy. Now, let's get you down to safer ground." Straight to business, he unclipped a helmet from his waist, put it on my head and fastened it. "Next, we need to get this sorted." He produced a harness.

My eyes widened in horror. With all the will in the world, no way could I have let go to put it on.

"Don't worry. You don't have to do anything." He shook his

head, as if already exasperated. "I can manage." He gestured to my midriff. "May I?" While I continued to cling on for dear life, Barrowboy began fiddling around my waist and nether regions to secure the harness in place. Pulling at it this way and then that to make sure it wasn't going anywhere, he attached a rope to make sure I wasn't either.

"Am I safe now?" I asked, my voice weak. Goodness knew what the man thought. Even to my own ears I suddenly sounded like a five-year-old.

"Almost. Just one more thing to do and we're good to go." He manoeuvred himself to my rear and strapped the two of us together. "You ready?" he said.

Feeling like a big baby in some sort of maternity carrier, I shook my head.

"You mean you'd rather hang around here all day?"

I could hear the impatience in his voice and again, I shook my head.

"Then you're going to have to work with me."

I pictured the man's stern expression. "Okay," I replied.

"On the count of three, I'm going to start walking backwards. I want you to let go and do the same."

I whimpered in response, trying to summon up the required courage.

"You can use your hands to steady yourself if you want to."

Realising I had no choice but to trust him, I told myself Barrowboy had done this hundreds of times before. I took a deep breath in readiness.

"One, two, three…" he said.

Keeping hold of both me and his rope, Barrowboy began digging one foot into the mountainside after the other, steering me back down towards the ledge.

The wind continued to blow a gale making it a bumpy ride, but I did my best to follow in his footsteps. "Are we nearly there?" I asked, my heart racing as I tried to see where we were going.

"Don't look down," Barrowboy said, as if I was daft. "Just keep doing what you're doing."

I felt a jolt as we, at last, reached the safety of the ledge. My legs turned to jelly as my feet hit terra firma and I couldn't stop myself from shaking.

"Come on, love," one of Barrowboy's colleagues said, approaching with a blanket. "Let's get you wrapped up."

"Thanks, mate," Oliver said to Barrowboy, while Frank barked and fought to get out of the rucksack.

Barrowboy nodded.

Overwhelmed with relief, I burst into tears.

CHAPTER 10

*a*fter taking me to their vehicle and assessing my overall condition, the mountain rescue team wanted me to go to hospital to get properly checked out. But feeling humiliated, I'd refused to take their advice. At the time, I just wanted to get to Number 3, Bluebell Row, pack up my things and run back to London where I belonged.

Having managed to talk me out of doing a runner, Oliver had taken me back to Aunt Lillian's cottage, dragged one of her armchairs over to the roaring fire he'd set, and while he'd gone off to make me some hot chocolate, I sat motionless, watching the flames dance around. Frank, who hadn't left my side since escaping Oliver's rucksack, had taken position next to me, ensuring his head stayed firmly on my lap. Still wearing my coat and wrapped in the blanket the mountain rescue chap had enveloped me in, my mind raced as thoughts of what could have happened flooded my brain.

I could still feel the fear as my hands became increasingly numb and my grip weaker, knowing that if I hadn't managed to hold on as long as I had, I could have fallen. I had better odds of winning the lottery than I did of landing on that ledge and I pictured myself bouncing off the rock face, grasping and grabbing as I tried to break my fall. At best I'd have been left battered, bruised, and literally broken – ribs, arms, legs, neck... At worst I'd have been dead. Sitting there, my life flashed in front of my eyes just thinking about it.

If I had lost my life that morning, I questioned what impact my passing would have had. Jules would never have been able to enjoy Christmas again. Not only would that time of year be forever associated with her best friend's death, I knew the guilt she'd have felt for persuading me to make the trip north on her behalf would be too much for her to bear. My funeral would've been a pathetic affair, attended only by Jules and Harry, I realised, and possibly one or two of my ex-dog walking clients if I was lucky.

A tear of self-pity rolled down my cheek. It seemed Jules had been right all along. Going off those numbers I clearly wasn't a people person by any stretch of the imagination. Apart from Jules and Harry, no one would miss me, such was the mark I'd left on the world. Or lack of. But at thirty-four years old, how did I even begin to change that?

"Here you are," Oliver said. Entering the room with a mug of hot chocolate, he held it out for me to take.

I quickly wiped my tears away. "Thank you," I replied, trying to muster a smile.

"Are you okay?" he asked, concern written all over his face.

I nodded, feeling anything but.

He sat down on the corner of the coffee table, giving me his undivided attention. "It's all right if you're not. Because that's a big thing you've just been through."

"Honestly, I'm fine."

He looked back at me, his eyebrow raised, making it clear he didn't believe a word of what I'd just said.

"Really," I said, reiterating. "I'm okay. I'm just feeling a bit sorry for myself, that's all."

Oliver gave me a gentle smile. "Why don't I sort you a bath?"

"That's very kind…" I indicated my mug. "But I think you've done enough."

"Antonia, I want to. Besides, it's the best way to warm you up." He smiled. "Or should I say, second best?"

I let out a laugh. "All right," I said, grateful. "A bath it is. Although if you do need to go, get to work or something, I can run one out later."

He headed for the living room door.

"It wasn't your fault, me getting stuck like that," I said, stopping him in his tracks.

"That doesn't mean I don't feel terrible about it," Oliver said. "Going up Fotherghyll Fell was my idea, remember."

As he headed upstairs, I knew it would have been easy for me to blame Oliver for the whole fiasco, but being honest, I felt bad that he felt bad. I'd known trudging o'er hill and dale wasn't my thing and I scolded myself for not asking what he'd had planned for us before agreeing to go. Not only that, I could have easily refused to continue when it finally dawned on me where we were headed. Just like I could have said no when it came to the point of having to climb some of the way instead of walking. I sighed. Poor Oliver was running around after me because he felt accountable, when he really had no reason to think that.

Wrapping my hands around my mug, I took a sip, immediately grimacing at the amount of sugar I could taste. Oliver was obviously trying to counteract any shock I might have gone into, and I found myself smiling again, thanks to his behaviour being as sweet as the drink he'd made. However, while I appreciated Oliver's efforts on the caring front, I also couldn't help but scoff at the situation. Never before had any man looked after me like Oliver was doing and as I sat there still shivering, I thought it a shame it took almost falling off a rock face, near hypothermia, and a chap's remorse for me to experience it.

CHAPTER 11

a full coal scuttle and pile of kindling at the ready, I knelt in front of the hearth ready to set the fire. Following the previous day's mountainside calamity, I still felt cold. And, I had to admit, humiliated.

My phone bleeped and twisting round, I picked it up off the coffee table.

Just checking all's well after yesterday. Here if you need me.
Oliver x

I squirmed. If it was up to me, I'd never mention the episode ever again and as kind as his text was, I put my phone back down, deciding I'd respond later.

While it was an experience I wanted to forget, I doubted others thought the same and I sighed, recalling how Barrowboy had said people were already talking about me. Being a new face in the village, I'd expected some chatter. But thanks to Fotherghyll Fell, the locals really had something to get their teeth into. I could almost hear everyone laughing at my expense – the feckless city woman clinging on for dear life, until mountain rescue stepped into the breach. My stomach lurched. I was never showing my face in public again.

I consoled myself in the knowledge that, thanks to technology, I didn't have to. Courtesy of the internet, in just one click I could get anything I wanted, delivered straight to the door, within twenty-four hours. In fact, what happened up that mountain was a godsend, I insisted. After all, it meant I could get on with organising my future as a roadside reclamation specialist, distraction free.

I reached for the box of firelighters but as I opened it, the whole of my upper torso crumpled. "Please, no," I said. As I stared into the empty box, it seemed internet or not, my self-imposed incarceration had ended before it had begun. I turned to Frank. "You know what this means, don't you?" I rose to my feet and headed out into the hall. "Come on, boy." Putting my coat on, I picked up Frank's lead, and as I led the dog outside, thanked goodness for everyone's Christmas trees. Blocking their view of the street, it meant there was less chance of anyone seeing us.

I walked fast, refusing to let Frank stop and sniff as we went. It was bad enough having to leave the house before enjoying at least two cups of coffee, let alone when it involved sub-zero temperatures and potential ridicule. "Bugger," I said, as I made my way along the icy path. Noticing a man lurking opposite the shop, it was clear the angels were working against me. I was about to be spotted.

I slowed in my step to observe him. A middle-aged chap, he wore jeans, a Barbour jacket, and a flat cap. He might have looked harmless, but the way he paced up and down was anything but. "What is he doing?" I asked, curious.

Scrutinising the man, I recognised him as the classic 1930s car owner from the other day. But gone was his jollity. He looked nervous and agitated, and with no one but the two of us in sight, was clearly talking to himself. I tightened Frank's lead as the man put a foot in the road, but rather than cross, he seemed to change his mind again. My frown deepened.

I told myself to ignore him. Where I came from, engaging with strangers wasn't the done thing. In a place like London, it didn't always pay to get involved. Despite any good intentions, people got hurt.

But you're not in London, a little voice said.

I reminded myself that less than twenty-four hours previous I'd been the one in need of assistance. And while my embarrassing experience on the rock face highlighted my stupidity amongst the locals, that didn't mean I shouldn't pay the help I'd been given forward. I sighed and telling myself I had no choice but to intervene, called out to him. "Is everything all right?"

My presence took Flat Cap Man by surprise. "Sorry?"

"Are you okay?"

"Yes. I'm fine. I was just..." As cheery as he sounded, his accompanying smile was less than convincing; his confidence forced. "I just wanted to..." He glanced over at the shop. "Anyway, must get on."

Watching the man stride away, I had to wonder what I'd just witnessed. I took another deep breath, puffing out my cheeks as I exhaled. Recalling Ted Sharples from the pub, and his strange behaviour, I couldn't help but wonder if Little Leatherington was home to any normal people.

Shaking my head, I put all thoughts of weird residents to one side and got back to the matter at hand. Scouring for somewhere to secure Frank's lead, I spied a bench at the side of the shop and tied the dog to it. Frank had never been one to follow commands and I knew from experience that he'd be off into the distance as soon as my back was turned if I left him to his own devices. "Be good," I said, heading inside for firelighters.

A woman, who I put in her forties, perched on a stool behind the counter. She had her head in a book so engrossing that she didn't look up. Although that was nothing to what she wore. I sighed, disappointed at the sight – a pair of deely boppers. My eyes went from her glittery Alice band, home to two reindeer heads, each wobbling about on their own spring, to the rest of the shop, searching for any other signs of Christmas about the place. There weren't any, just lines of tinned foods, a fridge for milk and dairy products, and a space for bread. Approaching the shelves, I looked back at the woman, confused, not knowing whether to admire her festive attempt, or question why she'd bothered.

After finding what I wanted, I headed back to the till. I waited for the shopkeeper to put down her book, but as I stood looking at her, she simply continued to read as if I wasn't there. I coughed. However, that was to no avail and wondering which book could hold her attention like that I craned my neck trying to get a look at the cover. I couldn't see the title, but from the image I glimpsed, it looked like a sweeping romance and knowing I couldn't compete with that, I stuffed the firelighters into my rucksack, dug out my purse and cobbled together enough change to cover the cost. Placing it on the counter, it seemed that wasn't enough to attract the woman's attention either. So I had no choice but to leave her to her reading.

I scoffed as I stepped out in the open air. "If Flat Cap Man was working up the courage to rob that shop, Frank, he needn't have worried." I began untying the dog's lead. "He could have emptied the whole place and the woman in there wouldn't have noticed."

A stick lay by Frank's side and as we set off, he picked it up.

"Come on," I said. "Let's get back before we come across anyone else."

"Settling in all right?" a male voice asked, just as Frank and I got to the door.

My heart sank and my shoulders dropped. Hiding myself away seemed to be proving impossible. As did getting on with work.

CHAPTER 12

*I*t would have been easy to pretend I hadn't heard the man and, instead, scuttled indoors. But ignoring the temptation, I put a smile on my face and spun round to see who the voice belonged to. "Yes, thank you," I replied. "I'm settling in well." Choosing to omit the fact that things could have been better, I took in the man before me. He wore a thick camouflage jacket, a woolly hat, and white trainers, while his massive grin and direct stare gave him an air of eccentricity. "Can I help you?" I asked.

"No," he said. "I just thought I'd say hello. And welcome you to the village." He stepped forward with his arm outstretched. "I'm Jason. Pleased to meet you."

I cocked my head, as all thoughts of local gossip, hiding away, and work-related research vanished into the ether.

"Jason?" I asked. Shaking his hand, I hadn't meant to sound surprised, but I was sure there couldn't have been two people with that name in a village as small as Little Leatherington. I told myself there had to be, because the chap before me did not seem anything like the handsome bad boy Jules had talked about. "Sorry. Antonia," I said, pulling myself together enough to give my name.

"I know. You're the one who got stuck up Fotherghyll."

I swallowed my embarrassment.

"I wouldn't worry. You're not the first person to need mountain rescue and you won't be the last."

I appreciated his matter-of-fact tone.

The man turned his attention to Frank, who dropped his stick in favour of the quick fuss he was getting. "Well you're a funny looker," Jason said, leaving me wondering if that was an observation or an insult. He looked my way again. "Did you know that San Fernando is the Christmas capital of the Philippines?"

"No," I replied. "I didn't know that."

"They hold a giant lantern festival. Every year, on the Saturday before Christmas Eve. Villages compete against each other to build the biggest and best lantern. People travel from all over the country to see them."

"Really?" As interesting as that all sounded, I couldn't help but question why he was telling me.

"It'd be great if we did something like that around here."

"I'm sure it would," I said.

"We can't, of course. Too much of a fire risk. Plus, lanterns would scare the sheep."

"There is that I suppose." My confusion continued.

"The cattle would be all right. They're indoors at this time of year."

Listening to him, I struggled to believe the man stood chatting and Jules's schoolgirl crush were one and the same. Recalling her wistful discussion, I didn't have a clue how to break the news to her that he hadn't turned out quite as she'd anticipated. In Jules's view, the Jason she knew was either a criminal overlord or running some billion-dollar tech firm. As far as she was concerned, he most certainly wasn't still living in Little Leatherington, talking about lanterns, and calling her dog a funny looker.

An approaching Land Rover caught my attention when it began to slow, before the driver brought it to a halt opposite.

I cringed, humiliation washing over me, as I immediately recognised the driver.

He wound down his window. "Everything all right?" Barrowboy asked. He looked from me to Jason, his face serious.

"Fine," I replied. Willing myself not to blush, I recalled him carrying me off the mountain in a giant baby carrier. "How are you?" I asked, trying to sound a lot more easy and breezy than I felt.

"Jason," he called out, completely ignoring my question.

Jason turned, while I wondered if Barrowboy recognised me. To say less than twenty-four hours previous, he'd saved me from what had felt like near death, he certainly wasn't acting like it.

"Time to go," Barrowboy said.

While I stood there bewildered, Jason headed to the vehicle and happily climbed in. He put a hand up and waved my way as the Land Rover set off again. Unlike Barrowboy, I noted, who kept his hands on the wheel and his eyes forward.

I stood there, wondering what had just happened. "Where the hell are we, Frank?" I asked, watching them go.

$\mathcal{S}$at on the sofa in front of a roaring fire and with a cup of coffee to hand, I propped my phone against a bowl on the coffee table and tapped to video call Jules. It felt odd not being able to pop round for a proper catch-up and not for the first time that day I thanked goodness for technology.

Her smiling face suddenly appeared on the screen. "Just a second," she said. Glue stick in hand, she was attaching a Christmas tree cut-out to a sheet of white paper. She had glitter in her hair and what looked like a shiny silver star stuck to her cheek. "I've decided to make better use of my time while I'm stuck in this chair," she said. "Instead of buying cards this year, I'm crafting some of my own."

With less than two weeks to go until Christmas Day, I couldn't help but think she'd left it a bit late.

Her tongue poked out of the corner of her mouth as she concentrated. "This looked a lot easier when the woman on the telly did it," she said. She was using her broken leg as a workstation; tubes of glitter, not all of them upright, sat with a pair of scissors, a pile of different coloured card, and a pack of felt-tip pens, on the section of cast that ran from her thigh to her knee. While I couldn't deny I'd seen less mess in kindergarten, Jules smiled as she held up her efforts to assess them. "Perfect," she said.

If I didn't know better, I'd have said she was enjoying her immobility a bit too much.

At last, she put the glue stick down and gave me her full attention. "So, how are you getting on?"

"Okay," I replied. "Apart from nearly killing myself yesterday."

She looked back at me, horror-struck.

I told her about my experience with Oliver. How I'd thought we were going sightseeing only to find myself hanging off a rock face. How mountain rescue had had to intervene and how I couldn't show my face in public again thanks to the shame. Any shock my friend felt fast disappeared. It was a debacle that Jules didn't just find amusing, she found it hilarious. The more I talked, the more tears of laughter streamed down her face.

"Enough," she finally said. "If you carry on, I'm going to wet myself."

I took in my friend's hilarity. "Jules, none of this is funny. I've never been so scared in my life."

"I'm sorry," she said trying to pull herself together, but the odd snigger continued to escape her mouth. "While we're on the subject of exploring..." She paused mid-sentence to reach down the side of her chair before producing what looked like a handwritten note. "I know you're not interested in what me and Harry had planned, so I've been doing some research on your behalf. There's a Christmas market on nearby. I'll send the details so you can check it out."

"Never mind that," I said, staring at her.

"You mean there's more?"

"No. I mean it's time for you to fess up."

"What are you talking about?"

"I'm talking about you breaking your leg on purpose. So you wouldn't have to come here."

Jules chuckled, clearly wondering where our conversation was going.

"You knew how weird this place is," I carried on. "So you threw yourself down those steps. Come on. Be honest. The rubbish bins had nothing to do with it."

Her laughter continued. "There's nothing wrong with Little Leatherington. It's a beautiful village."

"I can tell you've not met the locals recently." I picked up my drink.

"They can't be that bad." She reached down the side of her chair again. This time to retrieve her flask and pour herself a cup of coffee.

I scoffed. "Oh, they're worse than bad."

"Really. Knowing you, everyone's probably just being super friendly. You're a new face in town and they're making an effort. You should try it some time."

Drinking a mouthful of coffee myself, I almost choked. "I'm telling you. The local residents are seriously strange."

"How would you know? People aren't exactly your thing."

"Normal people are."

Jules let out a laugh. "You think? Antonia, the only friends you have are me and Harry. You avoid every other human being like they're diseased."

"I do not," I replied. Feeling indignant, I dismissed the fact that only a day prior I'd totted up my funeral numbers.

"That's why you worked as a dog walker, is it? Because you like to mingle with your fellow man?"

"I dealt with their owners too, remember."

"Barely." It seemed Jules was on a roll. "And what do you do when the dog walking stops?" she said. "Instead of getting a job in an office or a coffee shop, which London is full of, by the way, you buy yourself a knackered old van and become a skip rat. How's that for avoidance?"

"Roadside reclamation specialist, if you don't mind."

"Same thing."

As much as I didn't want to admit it, the incident on Fotherghyll Fell had already highlighted some of what Jules was saying. But I'd never been one for small talk amongst strangers or felt the need to have a big circle of friends. And whereas I'd always put that down to being an only child and simply being happy in my own company, Jules, who would talk to everyone and anyone, claimed I just hadn't found my circle yet. As for Little Leatherington, Jules had visited the place and therefore had to know how weird the residents were. I told her about Ted Sharples, the old man from The Cobblestone Tavern to prove my point.

"He's entitled to be grumpy," Jules said. "It's one of the perks of getting old."

I told her about Flat Cap Man.

"There's nothing wrong with a bit of quirkiness."

I told her about the woman in the shop.

"I wouldn't have stopped reading either if I'd got to a good bit."

I scoffed. "It was more than a good *bit*. Her eyes didn't leave the pages the whole time I was in there."

"What do you expect?" Jules looked at me like I'd lost the plot. "It's Little Leatherington. The woman doesn't have to watch everyone that comes in. It's not like down here where every other customer is a potential shoplifter. It's a village, Antonia, and in villages people operate on trust."

I stared at my friend. "Jules, the woman wore deely boppers."

"Duh. It is Christmas."

Jules had always had the ability to be positive no matter the situation. That was one of the things I loved about her. And opening my mouth to tell her about Jason, I couldn't wait to hear what spin she'd come up with to explain his behaviour. Closing it again, I thought better of it. Jules was my best friend and the last thing I wanted to do was spoil any fond memories she had of her childhood crush.

"It's why you're still single," Jules carried on.

"What is?" I asked. Only seconds before, we were talking about my trip to the village store and I didn't have a clue what the shopkeeper's headwear or reading habits had to do with my love life.

"The fact that you're not a people person."

Our conversation seemed to have gone full circle.

"I mean, when was the last time you went on a date?" Jules asked.

"I don't know. Six months ago?"

She tilted her head, knowingly.

"Seven?" I said. "Eight maybe?"

"It was twelve."

I should have known she was keeping tabs.

"And can you remember who you went on that date with?"

"Nope."

"Which proves my point. A genuine people person wouldn't forget. Good or bad, they'd recall some of the details." She paused, a mischievous smile crossing her lips. "Which brings me to Oliver Chase."

I narrowed my eyes. "What about him?"

"I might not have seen him yet, but he has a lovely voice."

I pictured Oliver's green eyes and warm smile. As nice as Jules thought he sounded, he definitely had the looks to match. "Is that why you gave him my number? Because he has a lovely voice?"

"No. I thought seeing as he's hoping to find us a tenant, it might be useful for him to liaise with you. Regarding the house."

I stared back at her, waiting for her to crumble and tell me the truth.

"Well, someone has to think of your love life, because you certainly don't."

The woman had no shame.

"Speaking of which, I think you should ask him out," she said. "On a proper date."

I let out a laugh. "Jules, I'm not doing anything of the sort."

"Why not?"

I couldn't believe she had to ask. "After yesterday? No chance. Besides, I've got more important things to think about."

"Like what?"

"I have a business to set up, remember. I have to sort out a list of all the tools I'm going to need. To research workshop facilities and look into website hosting. As well as sourcing actual stock."

"All work and no play makes Jack a dull boy, Antonia."

I let out a laugh. "You're the one who said I needed to take time out. To reassess my future, remember. Well, that's what I'm doing. I'm taking your advice. As for Oliver Chase, for all I know he could be as barmy as the rest of them."

"Carry on like this and you'll never find out," Jules said. "There's nothing wrong with having a bit of fun. See it as a Christmas romance."

"See what as a Christmas romance?"

"Your date."

Sometimes there was no talking to the woman.

"I can just picture it." Jules's expression turned dreamy. "The two of you, frolicking in the snow, sharing a mug of hot chocolate, chinking glasses of mulled wine... It'll be like starring in your own festive Hallmark movie."

My jaw dropped. Sitting in that chair with nothing to do but stare at daytime TV and make Christmas cards was obviously starting to take its toll. "Jules, there is no date. Not now and not ever."

My friend smiled. "We'll see."

CHAPTER 14

*A*fter speaking to Jules, I'd decided I couldn't live out of a suitcase during my stay and had spent the hours since packing up Aunt Lillian's clothes. The wardrobes and drawers in each of the three bedrooms were packed with her attire and while I'd begun with the sole intention of making a bit of room for my stuff, before I knew it, I'd got carried away.

It had been an enjoyable task. Getting my hands on so many beautiful garments, I'd spent longer stroking fabric than I had folding and bagging. The number of times I'd stood in front of the bedroom mirror, holding a dress or a blouse against my body to admire. From the swing pants featured in Lillian's photo, to dresses with full skirts that cinched in at the waist; from delicate paisley blouses, to power suits with padded shoulders; there had to be original items from every decade since the 1940s. Lillian had had such a sense of style and at ninety-four years old, even her later wardrobe was modern but with a mature twist. Nothing at all like my grandma used to wear.

When I'd told Jules what I was doing, she'd instructed me to give everything to charity and even when I messaged her to say she could get good money for vintage clothes like that, she continued to insist I gave them all away. She said, "Going through a hard time doesn't stop people wanting to look nice. And why should it?" She was right, of course. But when I considered how much it was all potentially worth, a part of me still thought she was mad.

Making my way out onto the landing with the last of the mountain of black plastic bags I'd gathered, I placed it on top of the others. "A job well done, even if I do say so myself," I said, taking in the fruits of my labour.

My next step was to source a local charity that might want them. A food bank that extended its remit to other essential items, or a women's charity, maybe. I wondered if I should ask Oliver Chase if he knew what services operated in the area?

A picture of Oliver popped into my head. His blond hair, green eyes, and gorgeous physique... I felt a sudden fluttering in my tummy and dismissing it as hunger, I checked my watch. I couldn't believe where the day had gone. Forget lunch; it was almost dinner time.

I headed downstairs to the kitchen and pouring myself a glass of orange juice, decided to drink it in the lounge. Frank had been particularly quiet, and I wanted to check what he was up to. I chuckled to myself, realising I needn't have worried. I could hear his snoring before I entered.

Thankfully, the fire I'd set earlier was still going, and Frank was taking full advantage. He lay stretched out in front of the hearth and as I watched the rhythmic rise and fall of his chest, it seemed he was so comfortable even my presence wasn't enough to wake him.

I headed for the window and looked out. From the cottage's front garden wall, to the main road, to the roofline of the house opposite, everything was covered in a glistening coat of white, courtesy of Jack Frost. Unlike in London, where the iciness would have melted come mid-morning, it looked blooming freezing out there.

I closed my eyes to absorb the quiet, knowing back at home I didn't have the luxury of such peace. If I stood in my window down in London, I'd hear incessant engine noise thanks to never-ending traffic. People would be shouting into their phones as they walked by and trains and tubes would rumble in the distance. And there was no forgetting the wailing police sirens...

Opening my eyes again, that morning's conversation with Jules ran through my mind. I couldn't believe she'd suggested I ask Oliver Chase out officially. The woman was constantly trying to fix me up with someone, even if her matchmaking did always end in disaster.

I'd lied earlier when I'd told Jules I couldn't remember the last time I went out on a date. In truth, I remembered every sorry rendezvous I'd had when it came to potential partners. Not that there were loads, but it didn't make the dating game any less hard work. Because in my view that's what it was. A game. Not that I'd ever understood the rules.

The number of times men had gushed over my quirky choice of career. Shunning the conventional and becoming a dog walker was to be admired. However, an outing or two later and their opinion would, for some unknown reason, alter and they'd inevitably ask if I'd ever thought about getting a proper job. I smiled to myself. Goodness knew what response my latest role would elicit.

Jules called me picky. Oftentimes cynical. I wasn't. She just didn't appreciate how many men out there were already taken and looking for an *adventure* rather than a relationship. She hadn't had to kiss so many frogs that she'd lost hope over the lack of princes out in the world. Not that I was looking for a prince. All I wanted was to be able to be myself and it was exhausting trying to meet someone who didn't hope to change me in some way.

Then there were the out-and-out strange dates to negotiate. Like the one Jules had mentioned. Having organised the meet-up for me, as soon as she told me what she'd done I knew it was a bad idea. However, Jules was convinced she'd found my perfect man, which came as no surprise considering she thought that about every guy she tried to introduce me to. On and on she went until, despite my better judgement, I agreed to go. It had been the only way to shut her up.

Landing at the restaurant to meet him, anyone would have thought we were appearing in a Christmas episode of *First Dates*. The room was full of dining duos, getting to know each other over a festive romantic meal. Mistletoe had been hung above all the tables, should diners wish to avail themselves, and the menu consisted of dishes like *Honeymoon Spaghetti* and *Loved-up Lemon Tart*. Like the blind date itself wasn't pressurised enough.

Looking back, I had to admit the evening started well. Giles Richardson had certainly made an effort on the clothing front, sat there in a suit as he was. He had the build of a rugby player, the face of a model, and the manners of a gentleman. I was impressed. Never before had any man risen to his feet upon my arrival, let alone pulled my seat out for me.

The more we chatted, the more we realised we had things in common and when he didn't have an opinion one way or the other when I mentioned my job, I began to think Jules might have finally hit on something. The wine flowed, which may or may not be the reason for him laughing at my jokes, but either way our evening seemed to be going well. So much so, I was tempted to excuse myself and nip to the ladies, just to ring Jules to say thank you.

Then he brought his mum into the conversation.

"You should meet her," he said.

I smiled politely, while my stomach lurched. It was way too soon for family introductions.

"You'd like her."

I was more than happy to take his word for that.

"You have the same eyes."

I swallowed, starting to feel more than a tad uncomfortable.

"And just like you, my mum's a real dog lover."

By the end of the night, I knew more about mummy Richardson than I did about the man I'd just had dinner with, and I felt way too creeped out to even think about letting his lips anywhere near mine when his gaze wandered up towards the mistletoe.

I decided there and then I was done with even trying to find the right man.

I shook my head, dismissing the memory. "And Jules wonders why I'm still single." I couldn't believe she wanted me to risk going through that again, except this time with Oliver Chase.

My attention was diverted when a minibus pulled up on the opposite side of the road, its doors swishing as they opened and closed. The vehicle set off again and as it pulled away, I spotted a little boy. Stood there in grey trousers, a thick padded coat that looked one size too big, mittens, and carrying what looked like a school bag, he'd obviously just got off the bus. Putting him at about seven years old, I thought him a bit too young to be travelling on his own.

He looked to his left and then right, before a worried expression crossed his face. After a moment he sighed and, sitting himself down on the kerb, he rested his chin in his hands.

I began to feel nervous on his behalf. Not only was he going to freeze out there, he looked tiny and confused and I knew I couldn't just leave him sat on his own. Anything could happen to him. Jules might describe Little Leatherington as a crime-free zone where everyone trusted everyone, but when it came to the safety of children, I wasn't taking any chances.

CHAPTER 15

$\mathcal{L}$ ike men, children weren't my area of expertise, but I knew I couldn't simply leave the little boy sat there. I couldn't just ignore him. I had to do something.

With Frank still asleep on the rug, I put my cup down on the windowsill and headed out of the room. Grabbing my coat off the bottom of the banister, I threw it on and buttoning it up tight, let myself out of the house. I paused at the kerbside to look first one way and then the other and with no approaching vehicle or individual in sight, I made my way across the street. "Excuse me," I asked the little boy, making sure to keep my voice gentle. "Is everything okay?"

The boy looked up at me. "I'm waiting for my mum." As he glanced around, tears threatened in his eyes, but I could see he was doing his best not to cry. "She'll be here soon."

"I'm sure she will," I replied. At least I hoped she would. Despite trying to take charge of the situation, not only didn't I have a clue how to handle children, it was way too cold for either of us to be outside.

Shivering, the boy wrapped his arms around his knees.

"Can I get you something to drink?" I asked. "Some milk? Or a hot chocolate, maybe?"

He shook his head.

"It's very cold out here. It would help warm you up."

Again, the boy declined. "I'm fine, thank you."

Despite his tender age, he reminded me of myself. I was the same, even as an adult, when it came to people I didn't know. Polite yet lacking in engagement. I offered him a friendly smile, aware that I should probably introduce myself. "I'm Antonia, by the way. I'm staying at Number 3 just over the road there."

The little boy looked at me once more, this time scrutinising my features. "Mum says I'm not allowed to talk to strangers."

I felt my heart melt. "And quite right your mum is too," I replied. I was relieved to hear he'd listened to his mother's advice. Firstly, because he was keeping himself safe and that no matter the inducement, he wouldn't be trotting off with persons unknown, never to be seen again. And secondly, it meant I didn't have to pretend I knew anything about computer games, comic books, dinosaurs, or whatever the latest craze happened to be. "It's all right," I said, taking a seat on the kerb with him. "We don't have to talk. We can just sit."

As the two of us waited for his mother to arrive, I sneaked a glimpse at the little boy. He pushed his fringe out of his eyes and looked so vulnerable and innocent. I knew all the emotions that were running around his head. Feeling scared that something had happened to his mum. Feeling worried about what that might mean. Feeling anxious in case no one else came to find him. Having been in the little boy's situation numerous times when I was a child, I'd experienced the exact same desperation. Except my worries played out in an emptying schoolyard, not at a bus stop.

I dreaded to think about the consequences if I hadn't been at the window to spot him getting off the bus. While I appreciated we were in a village where everyone knew everyone, it only took the wrong person to be passing through and puff! the little boy could have vanished. People of all ages disappeared all the time. I only had to turn on the news back home and some horrific event was being reported. Refusing to think about any more *what ifs*, I looked around at the stone cottages and surrounding green fields and soaking up the calmness around me, took comfort in what Jules had said about Little Leatherington being a safe haven.

A car speeding towards us broke the quiet. It screeched as the driver hit its brakes, bringing the vehicle to a sudden halt.

"Mummy!" the little boy said. His eyes lit up and he jumped to his feet.

I stood up too, while the woman grappled with her seat belt and hastily clambered out of her car.

"Seb," she said, racing towards her son. "I'm so sorry I'm late." She pulled him to her and kissed the top of his head.

I felt a lump in my throat as I watched the little boy wrap his arms around his mum's waist, before squeezing his eyes shut and hugging her tight.

"I got stuck in traffic and..."

The little boy loosened his grip. "I was fine, Mummy," he said, looking up at her. "This lady looked after me." He gestured in my direction. "I didn't talk to her though. Because she's a stranger. And I said no when she asked me if I wanted a drink."

His mum smiled down at him, before turning to me. "Thank you," she said. "I really am grateful. Coming out of work I couldn't believe how busy the roads were..."

"Christmas shoppers, no doubt," I replied.

"As much as I love this time of year, there are definitely downsides." She took a deep breath as if to gather herself. "I'm Lizzie, by the way."

"And I'm Seb," the little boy said. He looked at me all serious and as if trying to appear older than his years, and held out his hand for me to shake.

"Antonia," I replied, accepting his gesture, even if I had already told him my name.

"I would have called someone, but..." Lizzie shrugged her shoulders, as if resigned. "Well, it's just the two of us."

"I was happy to help," I said.

"I honestly can't thank you enough."

I waved her gratitude away. "You're here now. That's all that matters."

The woman hugged her son again and leaving them to it, I turned to leave, glad to be getting out of the cold.

CHAPTER 16

I hadn't been able to stop thinking about what could have happened to Seb if I hadn't seen him at the bus stop and as I stood in the bathroom brushing my teeth ready for bed, I could still see the little boy's worried expression when he realised his mum wasn't there to meet him. The relief on Lizzie's face when she landed felt equally disconcerting. She'd clearly been frantic and the fact that the woman had had no one to call upon in an emergency made me feel sad for them both.

As I rinsed my toothbrush under the tap, I knew my thoughts weren't the result of recalling my own childhood. No matter how many times mum was late picking me up, I'd never come to any harm. It was my adult life that that day's predicament had resonated with. Just like the low numbers attending my thankfully non-existent funeral, I had very few people to call on in an hour of need.

Thanks to Lizzie and Seb, I'd realised how small my support network was. The only people I could count on were Jules and Harry. But they both worked, which meant in an emergency like the one I'd experienced that afternoon, me and any child I might have in the future would be stuck. I shuddered. In a place like London, the repercussions of that didn't bear thinking about. However, I knew I only had myself to blame. Developing a support system involved building relationships, something I hadn't exactly put much effort into. I took a deep breath and slowly exhaled, dismissing my train of thought altogether. After all, it was daft to worry over nothing. Not only was I childless, having decided my love life wasn't worth the hassle, motherhood wouldn't be calling on me any time soon.

Finishing off in the bathroom, I switched off the light and made my way down the landing to bed. When I'd first arrived at the cottage, it hadn't felt right taking Lillian's room at the front of the house, so I'd opted for the spare at the back. Frank was already snoring when I climbed into bed. He'd positioned himself at the foot of the mattress and was out for the count, and listening to him, I realised just how dog-tired I was myself. Not that I understood why. I hadn't exactly exerted myself that day. All I'd done was sort through Jules's aunt's clothes, a task that had been a joy rather than a chore. I reached over to turn out the bedside lamp and as the room fell into complete darkness, I told myself the fresh country air must have been to blame and snuggling down ready for a good night's sleep, I immediately felt my body relax. Emptying my mind, I closed my eyes ready to drift off.

My eyes flashed open. *What was that?* I silently asked.

Convinced I'd heard a noise from the garden, I lay there straining to hear. My ears were met with quiet and after a moment I began to wonder if I'd imagined it. I listened harder to make sure, but there it was again. A shuffling about in the grass below.

I told myself it was probably a cat pouncing on its prey. Being in the countryside there had to be an abundance of mice around. It was the perfect feline playground out there. I was worrying over nothing, so I closed my eyes again and settled back down.

Cough! Cough!

I bolted upright. *Jesus Christ! That is no cat.* There was definitely *someone* not *something* mooching around outside. My pulse raced as the shuffling continued. Whoever it was, they were obviously having a good snoop about. They coughed once more, and my panic rose. For all I knew, they could've been looking for a way into the house.

I threw back the duvet and putting my feet on the floor, I felt my senses heighten. Frank, on the other hand, continued to doze. "Fine guard dog, you are," I said to him, making sure to keep my voice low as I tiptoed over to the window. If someone was about to break in, it was clear I was on my own. Frank hadn't lifted an eyelid, let alone barked.

With a pounding heart and shaking hands, I plucked up the courage to pull back the curtain a little and peep out into the garden. Forced to squint, as my eyes searched the darkness for the intruder, try as I might, it was too dark for me to see anything. Almost whimpering, I again asserted I was worrying over nothing, comforting myself in what Jules had said about Little Leatherington being a safe place. Not that that explained why I could still hear someone trespassing on Aunt Lillian's property.

Letting the curtain fall, I wondered if I should head downstairs to take a proper look. "But then what?" I asked myself. "A citizen's arrest?" Realising the intruder could have a weapon, my imagination began to run wild at the prospect of coming face to face with a knife, or worse, a firearm. I was, after all, in the middle of farming land, so there were bound to be a few shotguns knocking about the place. Having already had one brush with death, I thought better of it. But I couldn't just stand there. I had to do something, or at least get help. I hastened over to the bedside table and picked up my phone.

Ready to ring 999, I hesitated, wondering where the nearest police station was. With Little Leatherington being so remote, I guessed it was probably miles away, which meant I could've been murdered in my bed by the time the emergency services landed. For the second time that week, I pictured Jules and Harry opening the door to a Met police officer about to ruin their Christmas with news of my death and as my desperation built and the noises continued, it was clear I needed help sooner rather than later. "Well, you did say to call if I needed anything," I said, remembering Oliver's text. My hands shook as I quickly accessed my messages and clicked to ring his number. "Come on, come on," I said, waiting for him to answer. "Please pick up."

"Hello," Oliver said, sounding groggy.

"You have to come over. Now."

"Antonia?" He paused, clearly needing a moment to gather himself. "What time is it?"

"Never mind that. There's someone in the garden. I think they're trying to break in."

"What?"

Almost able to hear him jump out of bed, it seemed I, at last, had the man's attention. "There's a burglar." I looked over to the window. "Out there. They must have read Aunt Lillian's obituary somewhere and thought the house was empty."

"Shit! It'll be Clarabelle."

"Who the hell's Clarabelle?" I asked. Surely the village didn't have yet another local weirdo? "And why would she want to steal from a dead woman?"

"Stay where you are. I'll be right over," Oliver said, before the line went dead.

CHAPTER 17

I stared at my phone as Oliver rung off, wondering what to do next. Clarabelle was obviously cause for concern. Why else would Oliver have swung into action? I'd already realised that Little Leatherington had its fair share of strange residents, but to know one of them could be dangerous... That gave the place a whole new dimension. My heart thumping, I swallowed hard, wondering if I should just pack up my stuff, ready to leave the second Oliver landed.

I told myself to calm down. The woman in the garden could easily have been an elderly friend of Lillian's. I began to picture a poor old lady, out in the cold wearing nothing but her nightdress. Suffering from dementia, she'd become confused for some reason and was freezing to death as a result. Tempted to go and check on her welfare, I reminded myself that Oliver hadn't mentioned any illness, or that Clarabelle might be in distress. He'd told me to stay put. Dementia or not, he obviously considered the woman a threat.

Frank lifted his head and looked my way, before closing his eyes again and going back to sleep, while my mind continued to race.

I couldn't simply stand there waiting to be accosted so I grabbed my dressing gown and tiptoed downstairs. Careful not to make any noise, I headed into the lounge and crept over to the fireplace. I picked up the fireside poker and stole back out into the hallway. My heartbeat pounded in my eardrums, and as I sat down on the bottom step facing the front door, I prayed Oliver would hurry up and get there.

My ears pricked as the front garden gate creaked and I held my breath at the sound of footsteps.

"Antonia?" Oliver said, his voice hushed. "Are you there?"

I leapt to my feet and raced over to the door to let him in. "At last," I said, pulling him inside.

He stared at the poker in my hand.

"What do you expect with a madwoman on the loose?"

"I've called for reinforcements," he said. He indicated my weapon of choice. "That won't be necessary."

I followed Oliver as he made his way through to the kitchen. "What are you doing?" I asked, as he raised his hand to unlock the back door. Horrified he'd put himself at risk, I couldn't believe he'd venture out into the garden alone. "Shouldn't you wait until help arrives?"

He turned the key.

"Then at least take this with you." I held out the poker.

"Really?" he replied, as if I was the mad woman.

I took a step back. "Well, if you want to play the hero." I held out my hand, gesturing for him to go ahead. "Be my guest."

A banging on the front door interrupted the moment. "Thank goodness," I said. The last thing I wanted was Oliver getting hurt on my account. I ran through to the hall to let in Oliver's backup, but as I flung open the door, my expression froze. Instead of coming face to face with someone in uniform, I found myself looking at Barrowboy.

"Where is she?" he asked.

With no time for explanations, I took in the length of rope hanging over his arm. "Out back," I replied, starting to wish I'd not contacted Oliver at all and just rung the police direct.

Barrowboy strode past and made straight for the rear of the house. Closing the door behind him, I struggled to catch up. He possessed a steely determination, leaving me worried for Clarabelle's well-being more than my own.

"Here we go again," he said to Oliver.

"Oh, Lordy," I said, my fears really beginning to set in.

Oliver stood with his hand poised on the door handle. "You ready?"

"Don't hurt her," I said, eyeing the rope once more.

I stood there feeling helpless as Barrowboy shaped the length of thick cord into a lasso. "Go for it," he said, nodding at Oliver.

"Be careful," I said, as the door flew open, and the two men headed out into the darkness. No longer sure where my loyalties lay, I didn't know who I worried for more – the burglar or them. I stood back, squinting, almost too scared to watch.

Oliver flicked on his torch and within seconds Barrowboy had hurled his rope into the air. I heard feet scuffling and what sounded like muffled groans. Clarabelle was resisting, because the struggle seemed to go on forever.

"Got you," Barrowboy said, at last.

My shoulders slumped. It was over.

"Antonia," Oliver said, amidst yet more huffing and puffing. "I think you should come and meet your intruder."

Not sure my nerves could take any more, I took a step forward and, horrified, I looked at the burglar before me, taking in her big brown eyes. Clarabelle's mouth made a chewing motion and mid-munch she coughed. "But that's a cow?" I said, not for the first time wishing I'd thrown myself off Fotherghyll Fell when I'd had the chance.

Barrowboy looked at me like I was an idiot. "Of course, she's a cow. With a name like Clarabelle, what else would she be?"

I glared in response, questioning why, out of all the people in Little Leatherington, Oliver had to call him for assistance. "I'm a city girl," I replied, wondering what the man's problem was. "What people do and don't call their animals isn't something I'm an expert in."

Barrowboy shrugged, turned, and began leading Clarabelle down the garden, towards the workshop. "Cheers, Oliver," he called back. "I owe you a pint." As he disappeared through the gate and off into the night, the clippity-clop of cow hooves faded the further away Clarabelle and Barrowboy got.

"Merry blooming Christmas to you, too," I said.

Oliver burst out laughing, not even trying to hide his amusement. "I'm sorry," he said. "I should have told you."

"Yes," I replied. "You should." Wondering what was wrong with me, I couldn't believe I'd managed to embarrass myself in such a dramatic way yet again.

"If it helps, you're not the first person she's put the bejeebies into. Clarabelle's forever being mistaken for a prowler of some sort."

I flashed Oliver a look, letting him know that I didn't believe that for one second.

He laughed. "Honestly. No one knows how she does it, but she's forever escaping. And when she does, she heads straight for the newcomers. Every single time."

"Another of Little Leatherington's characters?"

"That's exactly what she is."

Still not quite believing him, I shivered, as the cold air suddenly permeated my dressing gown.

"I should go," Oliver said. "Let you get back into the warmth."

"No." I took a step back. "Please, come in," I said. "After that rather pointless SOS, the least I can do is offer you a hot drink before you go. It's freezing out there."

"I'd better not," Oliver replied. "It's late and I have work tomorrow."

I supposed he was right. Then again, no matter the time, would he really want to fraternise with a woman who'd mistaken a cow for a burglar? "No problem," I said.

"Rain check?"

I nodded. "Fine by me."

Despite arriving via the front door, he began making his way to the rear garden gate. He turned to face me, walking backwards for a moment. "Sleep well," he said.

CHAPTER 18

*C*up of coffee in one hand, I covered my mouth with the other as I yawned for the umpteenth time. I didn't have the energy to take Frank out for a walk and sauntering over to the back door, I let him out into the rear garden instead. After the excitement of Clarabelle's visit, my embarrassment over the whole affair had refused to let me sleep, leaving me tossing and turning for most of the previous night. I couldn't believe I'd humiliated myself for a second time. What was meant to be a quiet Christmas break was turning into anything but.

I took in the cloven-footed hoof prints ruining what hadn't been much of a lawn to begin with and cringed that I'd thought a cow was about to break into the house. I could still hear the baseless panic in my voice when I phoned Oliver claiming there was an intruder in the garden. I felt myself blush as I pictured him turning up to find me ready to defend myself with Aunt Lillian's fireside poker. Despite his reassurances that I wasn't the first of Clarabelle's victims, the man must have thought me an absolute moron. I sighed, knowing I was, no doubt, the talk of the village – again. Yet another reason for delaying Frank's morning constitutional.

The dog pootled back into the kitchen, while I dug his food out of the cupboard and poured some into his bowl. Setting it down on the floor, I couldn't help but scoff as he dove straight in. "At least one of us still has an appetite. Eh, Frank?"

My heart sank even further at the sound of someone knocking at the front door. "Great," I said. I let my head drop to my chest for a second, before straightening back up again. "Another unwanted visitor."

Leaving Frank to his breakfast, I dragged my feet as I headed out into the hall. I was unsure what to think when I answered the door to find Jason smiling back at me.

"Merry Christmas," he said. His smile broadened as he held out a box of chocolates, complete with a silver tinsel bow wrapped around them. "For you."

Narrowing my eyes, I stared at the offering, not sure what I'd done to deserve it.

"They're to say thank you," Jason said. "For telling us about Clarabelle last night."

"Clarabelle's yours?" I asked, as he shoved the chocolates into my hand.

"She certainly is. We own a dairy farm just outside the village. We couldn't believe it when Oliver called to say she'd got out again," he carried on. "That's the second time this month. Honestly, we should have called that one Houdini, not Clarabelle."

"So the chap with the rope? He's your...?"

"Brother," Jason said. "You'll probably know him as Barrowboy, on account of his job with mountain rescue."

I tried and failed to see the connection.

"You know? Because he's the one lowered down with the harness and stuff."

I still didn't get it.

"Anyway, it's his farm really. I just help out."

I struggled to reconcile the fact that Jason and Barrowboy were so closely related; you couldn't get two different personalities if you tried. Whereas one of them was friendly and weirdly charming, the other was grumpy and distant. "Well, thank you," I said of the chocolates. "To both of you."

"No worries."

Jason's expression suddenly turned serious and as he redirected his attention to the neighbouring properties, I wondered what was wrong.

"I thought you were here for Christmas?" he asked.

"I am," I replied.

"It doesn't look like it," Jason said, appearing genuinely confused. "Where are all your decorations? Everyone else has them up by now." He nodded to the window. "There's not even a tree. Lillian always had a tree."

"I didn't think to get one," I replied.

"Why not?" He shook his head at my failure.

If truth be known, I'd chosen to do without. Planning my new venture, losing myself in crap TV and reading a good book or two didn't call for all the festive razzmatazz. "I suppose it didn't seem like a priority."

"I thought it was just me and Barrowboy that didn't bother." Jason's expression brightened again. "We used to. When Mum and Dad were alive. We'd pin strings to the wall to hang cards on, and drink home-made eggnog. Mum made the best Christmas cake. I can still see her now, feeding it with brandy." He chuckled at the memory. "Talk about it packing a punch." His smile faded. "Christmas hasn't been the same since they passed."

"I'm sorry to hear that," I said. While I was happy to forego all the merriment and enjoy a quiet Christmas, Jason seemed the kind of chap who really enjoyed honouring the festivities. In fact, I readily pictured him giving Jules a run for her money given the chance. Unlike his brother, I realised, who I doubted let his hair down at any time of year.

"It's just one of those things," Jason said. "Barrowboy's too busy with the farm and I can't be trusted. Knowing me, if I even tried to cook a Christmas dinner, I'd burn the house down. It's safer to do without. And like my brother says, why go to all that fuss just for one day?"

"Why, indeed?" I said. Wondering if I had more in common with Barrowboy than I wanted to admit, I felt tempted to rush out and buy the biggest turkey I could find just to prove we were different.

"So where did you find Clarabelle?" Jason asked, his conversation flitting from one thing to another. "Round the back, I'm guessing."

I nodded, much preferring to forget the whole affair.

"She's too clever for her own good is that one. I've told her she'll end up in bother for it, but will she listen?" He laughed. "She probably takes after me. Back in the day I didn't listen either." He shook his head as if amused by his past. "Always out partying, dabbling in this and that, doing what people do at that age because, just like Clarabelle, I thought I knew better. That's how I ended up like this." He tapped the side of his head. "Good for nothing."

My heart suddenly went out to Jason. I couldn't believe he'd think that about himself, let alone say it out loud. Standing there stunned, I didn't know how to respond.

"There is such a thing as having too much fun, if you know what I mean?" he carried on, oblivious to my discomfort. "It's why my brain's addled."

Jules had said Jason was a bit of a bad boy back in the day, but I hadn't imagined anything as serious as substance abuse. Listening to Jason, I found his honesty shocking yet admirable. Whereas many would seek to distance or excuse taking drugs, the man before me seemed to own his past. However, that didn't stop me from feeling sad for him.

"That's why Barrowboy didn't want me talking to you the other day. He gets protective. People judge, you see. A lot think I'm either plain stupid or about to rob them. It doesn't matter that I've been clean for years." He smiled again. "I bet you thought she was a burglar, didn't you?" he said, suddenly back to talking about his cow.

I felt myself blush.

"Don't worry, you're not the first to make that mistake and, if Clarabelle has her way, you won't be the last."

"You mean she really does have form?" When Oliver had said that same thing, I'd struggled to believe him.

"Oh, yes. Not only is Clarabelle the world's greatest escape artist she's a fantastic mimic." Jason's pride in the animal shone through. "I bet she coughed, didn't she?"

"She did," I replied, surprised to hear him ask that. "It was the cough that convinced me there was someone out there. It was so human-like."

Jason puffed out his chest, clearly delighted to hear my response. "It's Clarabelle's party piece. She does it on purpose."

I narrowed my eyes. The man was obviously teasing.

"Honestly. Ask anyone."

I giggled at the thought. "It's okay, I'll take your word for it."

"Well, I suppose I better be off," Jason said, "and let you get on with your day." He moved to leave. "Enjoy your chocolates."

"I will. And thank you again."

Jason suddenly paused to say something. "Did you know that every Christmas in Gävle – that's in Sweden, by the way – they build a thirteen-metre-high goat in the centre of the castle square. They call it a Yule goat and have been building them since 1966."

"I didn't know that, no."

"Part of the tradition is for people to try to burn it down. Thirty-seven times it's gone up in flames, can you believe? Since 1966." He laughed. "Imagine that."

Watching him set off down the street, I shook my head. As refreshingly honest as Jason had proved himself, there was no denying his drug use had left its mark. I still liked the man though. Not only did I find him one strange cookie, I'd never experienced such a mind of useless festive information.

CHAPTER 19

The benefits of spending the day behind my laptop had been twofold. Firstly, I'd been able to start researching London storage and workshop facilities, even if the rents did seem to be outside my budget. And secondly, aside of my chat with Jason, I'd avoided all contact with, and therefore potential ridicule from, the locals.

Staring at a screen for hours, however, did have its downside. It had left me needing to clear my head.

It was already going dark when I decided to leave Frank at Number 3, Bluebell Row, and head to Wildeholt, a nearby market town and host to the Christmas market Jules had told me about. If I didn't check it out, she'd only nag me until I did. The trip over was a win-win; it would help me get rid of the brain fuzz and keep my friend off my back.

It wasn't that I was *bah humbug!* I just didn't go in for all the hullabaloo. I grew up in a house where Christmas acknowledged more than celebrated. While mum bought gifts and made a Christmas lunch, she didn't exactly go overboard with the festivities. She preferred a quieter affair. Of course, I knew that was down to circumstance more than choice, but her approach had rubbed off on me. Even when it came to my Christmas dinner, pushing the boat out for one felt both extravagant and unnecessary. Why go to the expense? Or the effort of chopping, peeling, dicing and slicing, when a ready meal had done all that on my behalf?

I scowled, as Jason's earlier conversation about Barrowboy popped into my head. It had been uncomfortable listening, but I refused to accept I was anywhere as near as festively challenged as his brother. For one, I couldn't imagine Barrowboy attending a Yuletide market under any circumstances. And two, when it came to Christmas, I at least put in *some* effort. I didn't write the day off completely.

According to Jules, Wildeholt wasn't a sprawling place; it was compact and pretty, with cobbled streets and an olde worlde feel. Narrow lanes, lined with leaning cottages and old stone town houses, led off the town square, which was home to various retailers catering for locals and visitors alike. Amenities such as a hairdresser, a grocer, a chemist and a post office, sat alongside cafés, a quaint little bookstore, and a fish and chip takeaway. There was also an outdoor adventure shop that sold everything a serious rambler or cyclist could possibly want. I chuckled as I parked up on Wildeholt's main car park. No matter what Jules said about making the most of the great outdoors, the latter was not a retailer I planned to avail myself of.

I grabbed my bag off the passenger seat and climbed out of the van. Not sure which way to go, I glanced around. There were lots of families and couples about, all of whom were heading in the same direction. All I had to do was follow.

As I got to the end of the street and turned left, the town square and festive market opened up in front of me. A huge, brightly lit Christmas tree towered above the wooden chalets from which vendors sold their wares and each chalet was connected to the next via a spider's web of fairy lights that went from roof to roof to roof. Christmas carols rang out from loudspeakers and as I began wandering through the market browsing all the goods on offer, the smell of gingerbread, roasted chestnuts, and spiced mulled wine floated on the air. From handcrafted jewellery and carved wooden toys to handmade soaps and candles, there was a range of products on offer, and all produced by local artisans.

The market's atmosphere was a sponge of Yuletide cheer. Vendors and browsers alike, everyone seemed to be smiling. There was a real sense of community, as people greeted each other and stopped to chat and joke like old friends and I felt myself getting caught up in the festive mood.

I paused to peruse a range of ceramic Glühwein mugs, each hand-blown and delicately painted by the stallholder herself. I knew Jules and Harry would love them. Practical and pretty, they were the perfect gift, and I couldn't resist buying them each one.

"Antonia!" a child's voice called out.

Surprised to hear my name, I spun round to see little Seb charging towards me. Trussed up like a chicken thanks to his thick coat, woolly hat and mittens, he also wore a big smile, and my heart melted a little at the sight of him.

"Sorry about this," Lizzie said, forced to catch up with her son. "As soon as he saw you, he just had to come and say hello."

"I've had a hot dog and some candyfloss," Seb said.

"Ooh, they sound good," I replied.

"They were. I wanted a toffee apple too, but Mummy says if I eat any more rubbish I'll be bouncing off the walls."

I laughed. Going off the little boy's excitement, he was one step ahead. It was clear the food additives had already kicked in.

"Do you want to come and watch me on the merry-go-round?" Seb asked.

"Seb," Lizzie said, clearly embarrassed. She nodded to the gift-wrapped mugs I held. "Antonia might not have finished her shopping yet."

"It's okay," I said to her, before turning my attention to Seb.

The little boy waited for my response, his eyes full of anticipation.

"I'd love to."

Seb jumped up and down, before throwing his arms around my waist and giving me a squeeze. "Come on, everyone," he said at last, letting go. I felt his little hand take mine.

"It's this way."

Lizzie shook her head as he began leading the both of us through the crowds, until at last, we reached the carousel.

I smiled and taking in the rotating platform and its row upon row of wooden horses, I felt like I'd been thrown back to my own childhood. I remembered thinking how beautiful their golden manes and pastel-painted saddles were and recalled how my tummy tickled with each rise and fall as the horses galloped. As a little girl, I'd imagine my horse breaking free of its mount, leaping off the carousel and carrying me into the distance to explore pastures new.

An unexpected pang washed over me, as I found myself wondering where that little adventurer had gone. When did she choose to keep going round and round without even a detour?

I shook myself out of it. I was being daft. Events of the last few days had had more of an impact than I'd realised and after everything that had happened, my emotions were bound to be all over the place.

"It's stopping. It's stopping!" Seb said, as the ride began to slow.

I smiled as he impatiently hopped from one foot to the other, eager to have his turn.

"He's going to throw up tonight, isn't he?" Lizzie said. She sighed in response to her son's excitement, resigned to the inevitable. "I keep telling myself thank goodness Christmas is only once a year."

I chuckled. "Coffee?" I asked, indicating the barista stand to my right.

"Ooh, yes, please," Lizzie replied. "At the rate this one's going, I'll need the caffeine to keep up." Trying to hold Seb back with one hand, she dug into her handbag with the other.

"Don't worry. I'll get it," I said, leaving her to settle her son on his horse.

The ride was underway by the time I got back. "There you go," I said, handing Lizzie her drink.

We stood in silence for a few minutes, watching Seb go round and round. He laughed throughout and frantically waved as he circled past.

I scanned the crowds around us, taking in numerous mums trying to stop their children from running off, while dads balanced toddlers on their shoulders. Couples held hands as they strolled from one chalet to the next, while others stared into each other's eyes as they sipped on hot wine. It was like a scene from a Christmas movie.

I filled my cheeks with air. A movie in which I didn't seem to quite fit.

CHAPTER 20

Dismissing the Christmas movie scene altogether, I wondered what was wrong with me. I'd always been an outsider. I liked being an outsider. Standing on the edge of other people's lives felt comfortable. Being the centre of attention did not.

Seb, however, had no problem taking the stage. "Yee-hah!" he shouted over and again at the top of his voice. "Giddy up! Giddy up!" His horsemanship seemed to be attracting quite an audience.

"Looks like I won't be putting my feet up tonight," Lizzie said, amused by Seb's antics just as much as everyone else. "It's going to be a bit of a struggle getting him to bed later."

A part of me envied the joy Lizzie's son brought her. Another part didn't. I might not have been a parent myself, but I knew the struggle people went through when raising children single-handed. "It must be difficult," I replied. "Bringing him up on your own."

"I can't say it's easy. We certainly have our hiccups." Lizzie chuckled as she looked my way. "Something you saw for yourself the other day." She turned her attention back to her son, her gaze softening as he rolled by once more. "But he's worth it."

As I took a sip of my coffee, my curiosity about their situation grew. "Tell me to mind my own business, but..."

"You're wondering where his dad is?"

"Sorry," I said, feeling myself blush. "I shouldn't have said anything. I'm just being nosey."

"He's in Leeds," Lizzie replied. "That's where we're from. Originally, the plan was for us all to move here. The three of us. I was to come first with Seb and settle him into school – which is what happened – while his dad worked out his notice, before starting a new job nearer to here. That bit didn't happen." She scoffed. "Apparently, country life wasn't for him, after all. And unfortunately, neither were we." She looked at me direct. "Let's just say he finds the company of his secretary much more entertaining."

I cringed, wishing I'd kept my mouth shut. The last thing I'd wanted to do was to stir up uncomfortable memories. "I really am sorry. I didn't mean to–"

"Please," Lizzie said. "Don't worry about it." She dismissed my concerns with a wave of her hand. "These things happen. We're almost a year on and, let's face it, I'm not the only single parent on the planet. There are millions of us."

As much as I admired Lizzie's stoicism, that didn't make her job any easier. Every lone parent out there had my admiration.

"Seb and I are fine just the two of us," Lizzie carried on.

"Mummy! Antonia!" Seb called out as he, again, galloped by.

Lizzie laughed. "Even if he does have more energy than I do."

The carousel began to slow, signalling the end of Seb's ride. However, before it had even come to a stop, the little boy was unbuckling his belt, climbing off his horse and onto his feet, almost giving his mother a heart attack by the look of things.

"Jesus," Lizzie said, doing her best to get to her son before he hurt himself. "That boy's going to be the death of *me*, never mind himself."

I let out a laugh and while Lizzie struggled to get on the carousel to rescue her son, I dug out a pen and piece of paper from my bag, before scribbling down my mobile number. "For you," I said, upon her and Seb's return. "I understand if you're not comfortable with it, what with hardly knowing me. And I am only here until the new year. But if you get stuck in traffic again, or need any help with anything, please, give me a shout."

Lizzie tilted her head and smiled. "Thank you," she said, taking the paper from my hand. "That's very kind of you." She indicated her son, who continued to Yee-hah! on what was a now make-believe horse. "Although I do understand if you want to change your mind."

I laughed. "Not at all."

Lizzie paused for a moment, as if wanting to say something, but wasn't quite sure if she should. "Actually..." She screwed up her face. "I know it's short notice, but are you free one afternoon in the next couple of days?"

I looked at Seb. Still on his imaginary steed, he skipped round and round in a never-ending circle.

"It's just that there's something I'd really like to get my hands on before it sells out. And now school's finished for the holidays."

Seb started neighing and whinnying.

Watching him, a part of me wondered what I'd let myself in for, while another part insisted entertaining a seven-year-old couldn't be that hard.

"I can ask his dad if you're busy," Lizzie said, clearly recognising my hesitation. "But it's not his weekend and he prefers to stick to the schedule." She lowered her voice, her tone suddenly mocking. "Or rather *Little Miss Secretary* does."

At last, Seb came to a standstill. "You mean you want to buy my Christmas present," he said, having obviously been listening. He shook his head, before turning his attention to me. "Mummy keeps pretending that Santa is real, even though I know he isn't."

"Santa *is* real," I said, feigning horror. "Keep talking like that and he won't be coming down your chimney any time soon."

The little boy looked from me to his mum. Taking in both our serious expressions, he appeared confused, as if no longer sure what to think. "But Samuel told me he isn't."

"That's one of his school friends," Lizzie said, by way of explanation.

"He said that parents just pretend he exists. So we'll stay babies forever."

"Well, you tell Samuel from me that he's wrong," I replied. "And that Santa will be very upset to hear someone's spreading such an untruth."

"You mean...?"

"I most certainly do," I said.

Lizzie was doing her best to keep a straight face. "Now do you believe me?" she asked her son.

Seb nodded. "I do."

"Good," his mum replied. Lizzie turned her attention to me, trying to disguise the amusement in her voice. "Now, about that afternoon..."

CHAPTER 21

 ith Frank laid in front of the fire and me having settled on the sofa ready for video contact with Jules, I clicked the call button and waited for her to answer. With just over a week to go, Christmas was fast approaching. A time when Jules would normally be high on adrenalin getting everything ready for the big day, I wanted to make sure she wasn't going stir-crazy for being stuck in her chair.

"Hi," she said, as her face appeared on the screen. She smiled and just like during all our previous calls, looked surprisingly happy to say she was still housebound. "Hang on a second. I just need to..." Her voice trailed off as her concentration increased.

"What are you doing?" I asked, taking in the sight before me.

She paused in her actions. "Knitting," she replied. Her forearms contorted as her hands wrangled with two long needles and a tangle of bright red yarn.

"I can see that," I said. "But why?"

She paused again. "Because I enjoyed making my own Christmas cards, I've decided to have a go at handmade gifts as well." Pride emanated from her as she held up her efforts for me to admire. "This is for Harry."

I stared at the woollen mass, unable to tell what I was looking at.

"It's a scarf," she said. "What do you think?"

Even with the clarification, I still couldn't make it out. However, I could see her face through its numerous holes. Wondering if they were part of the design, I thought better of asking – just in case. "Very thoughtful," I replied, instead.

"Of course, because I'm having to give your kind of Christmas a go... You know? Low-key and minimalist." Finally, she put her handiwork down. "I thought it would be fun for you to try mine."

"Excuse me?" I stared at my friend, realising I'd been right to check in on her. She might look fine on the surface, but underneath the woman had clearly lost the plot. No way was I playing hostess. On any day, let alone Christmas Day.

"Come on, Antonia. You might surprise yourself and quite enjoy having company for once. You could invite Oliver. And the woman from the shop. From what you were saying, she could do with getting back into the real world."

"Someone kill me now," I said.

"At least think about it. Call it a Christmas swap."

I closed my eyes, unable to believe what she was asking of me. "Okay," I said.

"You mean you'll do it?" Her face lit up.

"No! I mean I'll think about it."

"At least that's something," Jules replied, her frustration apparent. "So tell me, how are things in Little Leatherington?"

A picture of Clarabelle popped into my head and despite my better judgement, before I knew it, I was relaying the whole sorry tale. The rustling in the garden, the coughing, me stood there with a poker in hand ready to defend myself against a cow... Yet another Little Leatherington experience of mine that Jules found highly amusing. It wasn't long before she rolled with laughter. My friend's hilarity was contagious and although I struggled to completely rid myself of any bovine-related embarrassment, I couldn't help but giggle. Thanks to my friend, I'd at least begun to see the funny side.

Jules wiped her eyes with the edge of Harry's half a scarf, and finally, her merriment abated. "Oh, Antonia, you do make me laugh."

"It's not intentional," I replied.

"It was kind of Oliver to come to the rescue, though, wasn't it?" Jules said, not quite ready to fully move the conversation on.

The woman's tone and accompanying expression were loaded with unwarranted suggestion and I shook my head in response. "He wasn't there to help *me* as such," I said. "He was there to help Barrowboy recapture his cow."

"Please don't set me off again," Jules said with a snigger. She reached down for her flask and poured herself a drink. "Have you invited Mr Chase out on that date yet?" The hope on her face was undeniable.

"No. And I'm not going to."

Jules's hope turned to disappointment.

I could have thrown her a breadcrumb and mentioned the rain check Oliver had talked about, but I decided not to. Especially when days after requesting it, he hadn't called or messaged to renew my invitation. If the man had no interest in sitting down for a cup of coffee, he certainly wasn't up for what Jules had in mind for us.

"I could ask him out for you?" Jules said.

Horror swept across my face. "Don't you dare," I replied, aware that the woman was serious. "How old are we? Twelve? Anyway, you know me. I'm only here for a couple of weeks and I don't do casual."

"Antonia, when it comes to men you don't *do* anything." She gave me a knowing look. "Carry on the way you're going, and you'll end up like that old man you told me about. The one with the chair."

A picture of Ted Sharples sat scowling at everything and everyone in his immediate vicinity popped into my head. "Jules," I said. "I thought you were meant to be my friend?"

She carried on, regardless. "You'll be grumpy and unapproachable. And people won't want to share a table with you because you're too miserable to associate with."

"What? If I don't find a man, I'll turn into some cantankerous spinster?"

Jules laughed. "Of course not. What century do you think I'm living in? I'm talking about you not mixing with people in general. You might like your own company now, but there could come a time when it's no longer through choice. It'll be because you've turned into the female equivalent of old whatshisname. It's what loneliness does, you know. It sucks every ounce of joy out of you."

"Not long ago you were telling me he's entitled to be grumpy," I said. "Anyway, Ted Sharples aside, you'll be pleased to know I visited the Christmas market you recommended."

"You did?" Clearly surprised to hear that Jules's eyes lit up.

"I certainly did."

My friend clapped her hands in excitement. "I can't tell you how jealous I am. I'm desperate to get out and about. Did you have hot chocolate and marshmallows?"

"No."

"A glass of mulled wine?"

"No."

Her enthusiasm appeared to dwindle. "You must have eaten chips out of a cone?"

"No."

"But you bought yourself a Christmas gift, right?" Jules asked. "Like a tree decoration or a nativity set?" She stared at me, evidently anticipating at least one affirmative answer.

"No," I replied. "Why would I?"

"The real question is why *wouldn't* you?" She sighed. "I suppose there's no point me even asking if you sat on Santa's knee?"

I let out a laugh. "Definitely not."

"Of course, you didn't." She sighed again. "So, what *did* you do?"

"I picked something up for you and Harry."

Jules's smile returned. "Really? Can I see?"

"Nope. It's for Christmas. Besides, it came wrapped. Oh, and I offered to do some childcare."

My friend wrinkled her nose, as if I was suddenly talking in another language. "You did what?"

I told her about Seb and how his mum hadn't been there to meet him off the school bus, before explaining how I'd kept him company until a distressed Lizzie arrived.

"The poor little mite," Jules said. "As for his mother, no wonder she was frantic." Jules put a hand up to her chest. "Imagine if that happened here, Antonia." She shuddered. "He might never have been seen again."

"That thought had crossed my mind."

"Hang on a minute." Jules's confused expression returned. "How does any of this relate to the Christmas market?"

"I saw them there. Seb and Lizzie."

"And?"

"I offered to step in if Lizzie needed me to watch Seb again."

"So you've nothing festive to report, as such? You all just happened to be at the same place at the same time."

"Well, yes. But it proves I'm not the *complete* un-socialite you seem to have me down as."

"I suppose," Jules said, looking completely underwhelmed. "So how do you plan to entertain this little boy?"

"What do you mean?"

"Well, he's seven years old. Children that age need to be kept busy. It's not like you can stick him in front of a computer game, is it?"

"Not at all."

"You'll have to have a range of activities." I could see Jules's mind whirring as her organisation skills kicked in. "Young children don't exactly have a long attention span," she said, as if preparing to execute some military exercise.

I thought back to Seb's excitement at the Christmas market and realised Jules was right. The little boy had certainly been high energy. He might be cute, but he was also the kind of child to get his head stuck in railings or jump from the top of the stairs to the bottom to fly like Peter Pan. The last thing I wanted was to have to explain away an impromptu visit from the fire brigade or a ride in an ambulance. Suddenly aware of what I'd let myself in for, I began to feel a tad warm. I knew nothing about looking after children. It was one thing sitting next to Seb kerbside for ten minutes in silence. Keeping him occupied for a whole afternoon was a different story. "I haven't thought that far ahead," I said.

"Not to worry," Jules replied, efficient as ever. "I can help. It's not like I don't have any time on my hands. I'll do some research, find some suitable activities, and email them to you."

Grateful for the help, I wished I'd thought my babysitting duties through.

"Don't worry," Jules said. "It's one child. What could possibly go wrong?"

CHAPTER 22

*a*fter speaking to Jules, I'd spent hours scouring every cupboard, cubbyhole and drawer I could find in Number 3, Bluebell Row, hoping to locate a stash of board games, playing cards, or jigsaws. It was a pointless exercise. Aunt Lillian and I were clearly of the same ilk. It seemed little people weren't her thing either; there wasn't a child-friendly source of entertainment to be found. "Come on, Frank," I said. Making my way downstairs, I put on my coat and picked up his lead. It was time to give up. He needed a walk, and I needed a drink.

A knock at the door caught my attention. It felt a bit late in the day for visitors and putting Frank's lead back down, I wondered who it could be. I ushered the dog from the hall into the lounge. "You stay here, boy," I said and shutting him in, I went to answer.

Surprised to find a delivery man standing there, I took in the big white van behind him and the huge box at his feet. I knew I hadn't ordered anything; he'd evidently got the wrong address.

"Antonia Styles," he said.

I cocked my head, surprised to hear my name.

"Sign here." He held out a screen on which I needed to add

my signature using my finger. The result was unreadable, but the driver didn't seem to care. He simply headed back to his van, climbed in, and drove away.

Carrying the box inside, I felt a tinge of excitement. "What do you think this is, Frank?" I said, as I entered the lounge and placed it on the coffee table. It felt like Christmas morning as I tore at the wrapping tape and opened it. Staring at the contents, I immediately knew who the delivery was from. "Thank you, Jules," I said, unable to believe how quickly she'd swung into action.

I pulled out a Yuletide colouring book and a box of crayons. Then a crafting kit for Seb to make his own pompom Christmas tree, followed by a pack of festive stencils. There were DIY snow globe kits and a bumper pack of Christmas word searches, a sticker book, and a drawing pad. I couldn't help but smile as I reached for the final item – everything a little boy needed to create a nativity scene out of stick puppets. I let out a sigh of relief, knowing if that lot didn't keep Seb entertained, then nothing would. I grabbed my phone and fired off a text to Jules telling her how grateful I was and to ask how much I owed her. The same day delivery costs alone would have put a dent in her finances.

"This definitely calls for a drink, Frank," I said, heading out of the room to get his lead. "What do you think?"

Leaving Number 3 behind, it felt way too cold to be out in the open air and I moved fast, chivvying Frank along when he stopped to sniff the ground and nothing else. I'd been stuck in all day and looked forward to both a change of scenery and cosying up in front of The Cobbled Tavern's huge wood burner while enjoying a glass of wine. Even if that did include sitting amongst hundreds of artificial Santas.

The shop light shone out onto the street and as we approached, I spotted Flat Cap Man loitering opposite. "What is this all about?" I asked, watching him put one foot in the road, before changing his mind again. "Hello," I called out to him. "It's a bit chilly tonight, isn't it?"

My presence seemed to surprise him. "Certainly is," he replied, gathering himself. As the lights in the shop suddenly dimmed, indicating it was closing time, frustration swept across Flat Cap Man's face. He shoved his hands into his pockets and kicked the ground at his feet. "Have a good evening," he said, before he sauntered off, leaving me to continue on my way.

Entering the pub, I felt my shoulders slump, as I paused in the doorway thanks to the sight that met me. The peaceful surroundings I'd hoped for weren't to be. The place was packed. Again.

"Sauvignon Blanc?" the barwoman called out.

Her memory was more impressive than her outfit, I noted. She wore another festive sweater, except instead of a snowman, that night's had Rudolf the Red-Nosed Reindeer on the front. Gone were the flashing Christmas tree earrings, substituted with twinkling red baubles. "Yes, please," I replied, making my way to the bar.

"Large?"

I nodded. "That would be lovely." I watched her pour my drink. "Darts night?" I asked, acknowledging the crowd.

"Dominoes." The barwoman handed me my glass. "I'm surprised to see you in here," she said. "After the week you've had. First Fotherghyll, then Clarabelle. To be honest, we all thought you'd be on your way back to London."

To be fair to her, it wasn't like I hadn't been tempted.

I glanced around for a seat and my heart sank even further. Just like on my last visit to The Cobblestone Tavern, the only free seat meant joining Ted Sharples.

The barwoman gave me a sympathetic look as I paid for my drink and picked up my glass.

"You ready for this?" I said to Frank, making sure to put a smile on my face as we made our way over.

"Not you again," Ted said.

My smile dropped. "Great minds," I replied. "That's just what I was thinking." While on the previous occasion I'd been polite over seating arrangements, this time I didn't bother with any niceties. I simply sat down without asking, whether he liked it or not. I took a gulp of my wine, while Ted folded his arms across his chest. He seemed to be making a point of not looking at me. Probably because, unlike the last time, he couldn't get away with staring on account of me not hiding behind a menu.

With his gaze elsewhere, I took the opportunity to turn the tables and assess him for a moment. He wore a jacket, shirt and tie, and what looked like Brylcreem in his thick white hair. Even the man's beard was groomed. Were it not for his scowl, he'd have been quite a handsome chap, I noted. In fact, the man was so well put together, I couldn't help but question why he chose not to put the same effort into his manner as he did his appearance.

As Frank settled at my feet, I turned my attention to the rest of the room. Going off the lively throng, it was clear the residents of Little Leatherington enjoyed their dominoes. Wondering if Seb shared this preference, I made a mental note to ask the barwoman if I could borrow a set just in case. I felt my heart skip a beat. Spotting Oliver Chase at one of the tables, I raised my hand in the hope of catching his attention. My wave faltered. He was too busy chatting to Barrowboy and the rest of his friends to notice me. I sighed, resigned to spending the evening with Ted Sharples.

Continuing to observe Oliver, I reached up and smoothed down my hair, scolding myself for not making more of an effort. Then I scolded myself again. Since when did I feel the need to impress?

"Good looking lad, that one," Ted said.

Obviously relishing my discomfort, he nodded towards Oliver, who without warning, glanced our way, but while my smile grew, Oliver's suddenly vanished. He seemed to freeze for a second, before saying something to his friends, who, in response, all looked back at us.

"If you like that kind of thing," I said to Ted.

I pretended I hadn't noticed Oliver's behaviour. However, suddenly feeling awkward, I needed a diversion, so I picked up my drink and took a sip. Willing myself not to blush, I felt confused. Everything had seemed fine when I'd last interacted with him. My heart sank. Of course, it wasn't. The last time I saw Oliver Chase, I'd accused a cow of being a burglar. And on the occasion before that I'd almost fallen off a mountain. I sneaked another look at him. No wonder he and Barrowboy were having a tête-à-tête, no doubt, at my expense.

I thought about what Jules had said earlier about swapping Christmases, telling myself it was a good job I hadn't agreed. Goodness knew what she'd been thinking when she'd suggested it. Who the hell was I supposed to invite? Not Oliver Chase, that was for sure.

In need of another distraction, I drank a second mouthful of wine, before turning my attention back to Ted Sharples. "So, how has your week been?" I asked.

Ted looked at me like I was a mad woman.

"Better than the one before, I hope?" I said.

The old man still didn't answer, but I wasn't for giving up. "It's just that you weren't in the best of moods the last time we met."

Ted picked up his drink and continuing to ignore me, took a long hard swig. If I didn't know any better, I'd have said the man was thirsty. As it was, I frowned at his attitude. "Are you always this rude?" I asked. "Or is it just for my benefit?"

Ted harrumphed. "Who says I'm rude?"

"I do," I replied. "My friend, Jules, says you're entitled to be obnoxious because of your age. As if grumpiness is a badge of honour. I, however, don't agree."

"Some of us don't like small talk."

Neither did I but at least I was trying. I glanced over at Oliver's table, but while his attention was thankfully elsewhere, he continued to look uncomfortable.

"I suppose you think a person preferring their own company is a crime too?" Ted carried on.

I recalled my last conversation with the old man, when he'd accused me of trying to steal his chair and I'd accused him of slander.

"It doesn't hurt to be polite," I said.

"And it doesn't hurt to let a man enjoy his pint in peace."

Once again, my eyes were drawn to Oliver. I suddenly felt flustered as his serious face looked back at me and I quickly turned my gaze back to Ted. As he downed the last of his drink and plonked his glass down on the table, I willed the old man not to leave. It was one thing looking like an idiot in front of Oliver, but to be a billy no-mates as well...

Ted rose and instead of heading for the door, he proved me wrong and made straight for the bar.

"Mine's a large white," I called out, as I watched him go.

My words were met with a rather loud chuckle; the sight of Ted's smile almost knocking me off my chair. However, it seemed I wasn't the only one to clock his grin and realising the room had quietened somewhat, I cautiously took in my surroundings. I felt myself redden, thanks to the numerous people staring at me. Including Oliver Chase.

CHAPTER 23

*A*t last, I had the table to myself. While Ted turned out to be better company than I'd anticipated, our conversation had still been stilted, which meant I'd had to do most of the work.

To be fair to Ted, he'd shared snippets of his life. Like the fact that he was Little Leatherington born and bred and that his wife had sadly passed away some years ago. I smiled, recalling how his eyes had lit up and his voice softened when he talked about her. The man clearly still loved and missed his wife, making me think he wasn't the complete ogre he portrayed himself as. I sipped on my drink and I mulled over Jules's comment about how loneliness sucks the joy out of people. What I now knew about Ted could've certainly explained his attitude.

Checking my watch, I supposed Frank and I should probably have been getting back to Number 3.

"Mind if I join you?" a man's voice said.

I froze. Lost in my thoughts, I hadn't seen Oliver approach. The man had to be kidding; I wished he'd go away. In contrast, Frank jumped to his feet and wagged his tail to welcome Oliver.

Traitor, I silently said. Although when it came to the prospect of getting attention, I had to admit the dog had never had a problem shifting his allegiance.

"Hello, boy." Oliver crouched down to Frank's level and ruffled his fur. "How've you been?"

Responding in his usual way, the dog flung himself down on his back in anticipation of a belly rub, clearly more than happy to lie there with his tongue dangling out the side of his mouth, while Oliver did his bidding.

Attractive, I thought, wishing the dog would get back on all fours so we could leave.

At last, Oliver straightened himself up, at the same time indicating Ted's empty chair. "Do you mind?" he asked.

The man's presence wasn't just unwanted, it was surprising considering the number of times he'd frowned at me that evening. But gone was Oliver's seriousness; his smile couldn't have been bigger. My eyes narrowed as I questioned what he thought he was playing at. Not that it mattered. Whatever his game, I had no intention of joining in. "And if I say no?" I replied.

He sat down anyway. "It's great to see you," he said.

I couldn't believe what I was hearing.

"I would've come over sooner."

I didn't believe that for one second.

"But you were busy chatting." He smiled. "I don't know what you were talking about, but that grumpy old man hasn't laughed publicly in years."

"He hardly laughed," I replied.

"Believe me, in Ted Sharples's world, he did."

I looked at Oliver, wondering what *that grumpy old man* had ever done to him. "I'd prefer it if you could be a little more respectful," I said. "Ted has been through a lot, what with losing his wife."

Oliver looked back at me with a twinkle in his eye. He clearly found my request amusing. He nodded to my glass. "Can I get you a drink? Another glass of wine?"

I shook my head. "I'm fine, thank you." My stern response seemed to confuse Oliver, but I didn't care. As far as I was concerned, the man had only joined me because the group he'd been with had left and talking to the mad cow mountain woman was better than talking to himself. I glanced over to where he'd been sitting to see his friends still there. Suddenly, Oliver wasn't the only one feeling bewildered. I was too.

"Is everything all right?" Oliver asked, following my gaze.

My attention went from his friends to him. If looks could kill he'd have hit the floor. "You really have to ask?" I said.

Concern swept across his face. "Antonia, have I done something to offend you?"

My eyes widened at the man's gall and as he continued to feign innocence, my annoyance levels rose. "Unless you're going to tell me you have a medical condition, then yes, you have."

"A medical condition?"

"One that affects your facial muscles?"

He leaned forward and put his arms on the table, continuing his charade. "Antonia, you've lost me."

"Look, I get that you think I overreacted the other night. That I should have known the difference between a cow and an actual person. I get that I'm not outdoorsy and can't climb your precious mountain. I can even accept that you'll be dining out on the back of both those things for years to come. But that doesn't give you the right to make me feel uncomfortable."

"Uncomfortable?"

"You could have just ignored me," I said. "Pretended I wasn't here. You didn't have to keep frowning as if my mere presence offended you."

"Frowning?"

I bristled at his response. "Please stop repeating my words."

Oliver laughed, an action that did nothing to soothe my frustration. "Antonia, I wasn't looking at you."

"Yeah, right." I folded my arms tight across my chest.

He laughed some more. "Honestly. I was looking at Granddad."

I froze again. "Granddad?"

"Yes. Granddad."

I whimpered, unable to believe I'd just told Oliver to show his own relative more respect.

"I know how grumpy he can be. I was checking he was being nice."

"Nice?"

"Now who's repeating things. Anyway, I was obviously worrying about nothing. The two of you seemed to be getting on pretty well."

I tried to get my head around what I was hearing. "So you *weren't* giving me dirty looks?"

"No. Why would I?"

Again, I looked at him like he had to ask.

Oliver appeared genuinely shocked. "If you're still hung up about Clarabelle, I told you she has a history of getting out and scaring people. Ask anyone here." He threw his arms out as if emphasising his point. "She's well known for it. And even if she wasn't, I wouldn't judge you for a genuine mistake. As for Fotherghyll Fell... Loads of people get stuck."

Despite Oliver's protests of innocence, I still wasn't sure whether to believe him. "And Ted's really your grandfather?"

"Yes, he is."

I stared at Oliver and comparing the two men's features I began to see a resemblance. They had similar shaped eyes and thick heads of hair. Although personality wise, grandfather and grandson couldn't have been more different. In fact, thanks to my outburst, I realised *I* had more in common with Ted than Oliver did. I cringed at the thought. As if I wasn't embarrassed enough, now I really wanted the ground to swallow me whole.

"And for your information I wasn't scowling at Granddad either," Oliver said. "I was willing him not to show me up. You've seen for yourself how abrupt he can be when he's feeling that way."

I swallowed hard, knowing I'd made a fool of myself and for the third time. My stomach churned as I realised I had yet another story to cheer Jules up with.

Sitting there, I knew I should apologise, but my pride wouldn't let me. "Well that's all right then," I said, picking up my glass and drinking a mouthful of wine.

CHAPTER 24

One week until Christmas

*T*hinking Seb could use the coffee table as a workstation, I'd piled all of Jules's Christmas activities on the floor next to it, along with a few extras that I'd picked up after squeezing in a second visit to Wildeholt, such as a glue stick, child-friendly scissors and pencils. And I'd got in snacks should hunger strike – fruit, nuts, and more than a couple of sweet treats, which were ready and waiting in the kitchen. "What do you think, Frank?" I said. "Enough to keep an active little boy happy?"

A knock at the door told me Lizzie and Seb had arrived and heading to let them in, I couldn't deny I felt a little nervous. But what I lacked in experience I made up for in enthusiasm. Besides, looking after a seven-year-old couldn't be that difficult, I insisted, before plastering a welcoming smile on my face and opening the door to greet them.

My smile vanished and I stood there confused. With no one

in sight, it appeared my visitor was a Christmas tree.

"For you," Jason said, calling out from behind its branches. "I saw you still hadn't got one and because Lillian's doesn't look the same without, we thought we'd surprise you."

As I took in the mass of greenery, I was surprised all right. The tree was humongous.

"Jason's idea," Barrowboy said, denying any responsibility for the situation I found myself in.

"I don't know what to say," I replied. The gesture might have been appreciated, but as someone who had a *less is more* approach to Christmas, I couldn't say the tree experience was wholly pleasurable.

"You might want to move out of the way," Jason said. "So we can get it in."

Good luck trying! I thought.

I stood aside, as Barrowboy manoeuvred the boughs so Jason could squeeze his way into the hall and while one pulled, the other pushed in their efforts to force the tree through the front door. After lots of huffing and puffing, Barrowboy also came into view and wrapped up in thick coats and woolly hats as they were, the two of them looked hot and bothered. Forcing the tree as far as they had seemed like enough of a feat, and they still had to get it into the lounge.

Finally, they managed it, but whereas Jason was pleased with their progress, his brother frowned. "The things you make me do," he said, hissing rather than speaking.

"We'll put it in the window," Jason said, seemingly oblivious to Barrowboy's annoyance.

"It's as good a place as any," I replied, forced to pretend I, too, hadn't noticed Barrowboy's tone. Staring at the carpet of pine needles in their wake, I wondered how I was going to get them all up. And as I watched them continue in their struggle, I flinched, hoping against hope that they didn't knock over one of Aunt Lillian's ornaments, or scratch her furniture.

Keeping hold of the greenery with one hand, Jason reached inside his coat with the other and pulled out a metal stand. He tossed it down onto the floor in readiness. "What do you think?" Jason said, as they at last secured the tree in position. He stood back to admire their efforts, clearly delighted with the result.

I, however, stood wide-eyed and silent. The tree almost touched the ceiling and was roughly as wide as it was tall. Light from the window struggled to penetrate its branches, leaving the room dark and dingy. "It's very commanding," I said, at least trying to sound positive.

"That's one way of putting it," Barrowboy said, clearly taking a less charitable stance.

Frank let out a whine and headed out of the room.

"I think it's great," Jason said, his enthusiasm more than making up for any shortfall.

"Antonia?" Lizzie called out.

We all turned as she popped her head into the room with Seb in tow. "The door was open, so I thought..." As she stepped forward her eyes automatically focused on the tree. She stood there, clearly trying to organise her thoughts before letting herself speak.

In contrast, her son knew exactly what to say and letting go of Lizzie's hand, he raced over to touch the branches. "Wow!" the little boy said. "This is one heck of a Christmas tree."

"Seb! Language, please," Lizzie said, scolding him.

Much to my surprise, Barrowboy let out a burst of laughter. The crow's feet around his eyes deepened and for once his smile appeared to be one of amusement rather than scorn. Watching him ruffle the little boy's head, it was a revelation to know the man had a softer side underneath all his gruffness.

"He's just saying it like it is," Barrowboy said. As his and

Lizzie's eyes met, Barrowboy quickly pulled off his hat and ran his fingers through his short mousy hair. It was evident that the flush in the man's cheeks no longer had anything to do with the exertion he'd been put through.

Astonished, I followed his gaze, noting that Lizzie was a little on the pink side too; and her rosy cheeks clearly had nothing to do with her son's outburst. As my eyes flitted from one to other, it was as if the rest of us weren't there. Had a child not been present, I'd have told them to get a room.

"I should get going," Lizzie said, continuing to blush as she turned her attention to me.

"Yes, we should go too." Barrowboy might have been talking to Jason, but he obviously struggled to take his eyes off Lizzie.

I wasn't the only one to notice the attraction between them. Sharing a knowing look, Jason and Seb giggled, having obviously clocked it as well.

"Good idea," I said, raising my voice slightly. "Seb and I have things to do."

"Are you sure you don't mind?" Lizzie said, getting back to the matter at hand. "He can be a bit of a handful when he wants to be."

"Of course, I don't mind," I replied. "We're going to have fun, aren't we, Seb?"

"I'd say yes, looking at that lot." He indicated the pile of Christmas activities awaiting his attention.

"Oh, let me give you this before I forget," Lizzie said. She fumbled in her coat pocket before producing a scrap of paper. "It's my number. In case of an emergency." As she handed it over, the woman appeared torn. It was obvious she wasn't used to leaving her son in someone else's care and seemed reluctant to leave.

I softened my tone appreciating her position. "He'll be fine," I said, giving her arm a reassuring rub.

"Jason," Barrowboy said, nodding to the door. He seemed to be back to his usual self too.

Jason looked from his brother to me and just like Lizzie, he seemed hesitant.

I had an idea why. As Jason fleetingly looked at the pile of activities, it was clear he wanted to join in the fun. I recalled our conversation when he explained that he and his brother no longer celebrated Christmas and, while he might not admit it, that obviously bothered him. I considered his kindness in making sure I didn't go without a tree even though he had to himself. "You're welcome to stay," I said, deciding that was the least I could do.

"Really?" Jason replied. He turned to his brother in eager anticipation, but Barrowboy didn't appear as keen.

I knew Barrowboy was only looking out for Jason. After all, Jason had told me his brother tended to be protective. Jason might be a grown man, but the damage caused in his past was evident. It had made him almost childlike.

"It's all right with me," Lizzie said.

Barrowboy seemed surprised.

"And I'd appreciate the help," I said.

"Me too," Seb said. He began sifting through the activities that Jules had had delivered. "Some of these look pretty tricky."

"Only if you're sure," Barrowboy said, still wary.

Wearing great big smiles, Jason and Seb high-fived, while I showed Lizzie and Barrowboy out, before they could change their minds.

Barrowboy paused at the front door and turned to look at me. "Thank you," he said.

CHAPTER 25

*H*aving seen Lizzie and Barrowboy to the door, I stood watching them for a minute. It was obvious the two of them were attracted to each other and I couldn't help but smile as they headed to their respective vehicles. Walking side by side, they seemed to be making a point of keeping a reputable distance, all the while sneaking glances when the other wasn't looking. I might not have been up for a spot of Christmastime romance, but it looked like those two were. Barrowboy's Land Rover was parked behind Lizzie's little run-around and seeing them stop to chat, I hoped they were about to swap numbers. Not that I hung around to find out. I left them to it and went inside.

Making my way to the lounge, I tiptoed through the pine needles, knowing it was going to be one hell of a job getting them up. Jason and Seb were already chatting, and I stood in the doorway watching and listening as they looked through Jules's activities.

"Do you know that Toronto heralds Christmas with a cavalcade of lights?" Jason asked the little boy.

Seb paused in his browsing. "Where's Toronto?" he asked, curious.

"In Canada."

"Near America?"

"That's the one," Jason replied, ready to carry on with his story. "Anyway, the first cavalcade took place in 1967."

Seb cocked his head again. "What's a cavalcade?"

"It's like a procession."

I smiled at Jason's patience and at how cute their interaction was.

"Initially, it was to show off their newly built City Hall and some fancy square. But they've carried on with it ever since. They have a huge Christmas tree and the whole area is lit up with more than 300,000 LED lights."

Seb's eyes widened at the number. "Wow! Is the tree as big as this one?" He pointed to mine in the window.

"Bigger," Jason said.

"Double wow! That is big."

"The lights are on every evening until the New Year. And they have firework shows and ice skating."

I shook my head, not for the first time wondering where Jason got all his Christmas facts. He seemed to be a mine of information on worldwide festive traditions.

"I can't wait to help Antonia decorate her tree," Seb said.

"Neither can I," Jason said.

"I bet we'll need 300,000 lights like in Toronto," Seb said.

I stepped into the room. "Sorry, guys, I'm afraid that won't be happening."

"What do you mean?" they both asked simultaneously.

"I don't have any decorations."

Seb looked my way, his expression confused. "You must have. A Christmas tree isn't a Christmas tree without tinsel and stars and baubles."

"Mine are in London," I said, matter of fact. "Where I live." I stared at the tree dominating the room, realising that even if they weren't, I didn't have anywhere near enough frills to brighten up that humongous evergreen. Back home, my tree consisted of a couple of frosted branches donated to me by the florist, tied together with twine, and adorned with a string of fairy lights.

Seb stared at the mass of bare branches. "But it looks so sad."

Jason sighed. "It certainly does."

They were right, of course. But as pitiful as it was, there was nothing I could do to change that.

The little boy's bottom lip began to quiver. "And lonely."

I couldn't help but think Seb was overreacting.

Tears welled in his eyes. "It needs an angel to keep it company."

"It needs something," Jason said.

I hastily joined them at the coffee table, eager to divert the seven-year-old's attention. "Why don't we have a go at making a snow globe instead?" I said. Desperate, I reached down and picked up the relevant box. "This looks much more fun."

"I want to make the tree happy," the little boy said.

"But if I don't have any decorations," I replied, hoping he'd see reason, "what can I do?"

"I bet there's a stash of them here somewhere," Jason said. "There has to be."

The man wasn't helping.

"How about some colouring?" I said, reaching for the crayons. I looked from Jason to Seb, but neither of them were impressed. A tiny sob escaped Seb's mouth and taking in the little boy's heartbreak, I couldn't understand how a discussion about a tradition that took place thousands of miles away in Toronto could have deteriorated so quickly. I felt at a loss. Having scoured the house for toys and puzzles, I hadn't seen anything at all that might help me turn the situation around. I began to panic. Lizzie hadn't been gone five minutes and I'd already made her son cry. If I didn't do something, goodness knew what state he'd be in by the time she returned.

"The loft," Jason said, somewhat randomly.

"What about it?" I replied.

"Isn't that where most people keep their Christmas stuff?"

I stared at Jason, hoping he didn't really expect me to climb all the way up there.

He looked at me expectantly, his expression telling me that yes, he did.

My gaze went from him to Seb, and with both willing me to at least go and check, I realised I was never going to get any peace unless I did just that. I sighed. "Okay," I said. "Let's go and have a look. But if we can't find any, we make the snow globe instead."

My two guests smiled. "Deal!" they both said.

They were right behind me as I headed out into the hall, trudged up the stairs and grabbed a chair from Aunt Lillian's bedroom. I placed it on the landing under the entrance to the loft, but before I'd even tried to stand on it visions of Fotherghyll Fell flooded my mind. I hesitated and my hands shook as I steeled myself for the task at hand. I lifted my foot onto the seat before, much to my relief, Jason put his hand out to stop me.

"Let me," he said, clearly recognising my plight. He climbed up onto the chair, opened the hatch, and pulled on the ladder above. Forced to keep hold of the bottom rung with one hand, he easily leapt off the chair and manoeuvred it out of the way to make room for the ladder to extend downwards. "Do you want me to do the search as well?" he asked.

I nodded, grateful, as Jason made the ascent.

"It's a bit dark up here... Hang on a minute. I think I've found a light."

"What can you see?" I asked, as the space above illuminated. "Lots of boxes."

I wasn't surprised to hear that going off the rest of the house. "But they're all labelled."

The sound of cardboard being slid around the loft floor filtered down, as Jason shifted box after box, while Seb stared upwards, his expression hopeful.

"Found them," Jason said, at last.

"Yay!" Seb clapped his hands as he hopped from one foot to another, while Jason began climbing down the ladder, expertly negotiating the packed Christmas decorations through the hatch above his head.

I stepped forward, my arms upstretched to ease the box down and once his feet were safely on terra firma, Jason pushed the loft ladder up, returning it to its original position.

"I won't bother locking it," he said. "So we can put the box back when we're done."

"Now the tree will look happy," Seb said, as we all made our way downstairs.

Jason placed the box on the lounge floor and his and Seb's eyes were full of anticipation as they waited for me to open it. Reaching down, I surprised myself by feeling the same. Jules's aunt had so many wild and wonderful trinkets and souvenirs from her travels, I could only imagine what treasures were waiting to be revealed.

"What about music?" Seb said, stopping me in my tracks. "Me and Mummy always play Christmas songs when we decorate our tree."

"How could I forget?" I said, feigning horror. I pulled my mobile out of my pocket and searched YouTube for a Christmas playlist. Opting for the first one that appeared on the screen, I hit the play button and turned up the volume. As "Jingle Bells" began to ring out, Jason and Seb sang along as we unpacked the box, their eyes widening at the delights before them.

We found a travelling Father Christmas who, instead of wearing red, wore grey and carried a golden lantern to light his way. There was a set of silver bell baubles, each unique in pattern and sound and of course, Seb insisted on ringing each and every one before finding them a place on the tree. Making sure to handle them with care, Jason hung a selection of coloured glass baubles. Some had reflectors, while others were patterned in glitter. There were little doe-eyed papier mâché reindeer, and red and white porcelain candy canes. Ribboned hearts were hand-painted with snowy village scenes, and there was no tinsel, but long strings of wooden beads in red and yellow were the perfect replacement. Finally, Seb and Jason wound fairy lights all around the tree's branches.

"Who's doing the honours?" I asked, indicating the adaptor switch.

Jason nodded that Seb should go ahead.

"Really?" the little boy said. He raced over and pressed the button, delighted with himself when the tree lit up in all its glory.

Not usually one to fawn over such things, even I couldn't deny the tree looked wonderful. Thanks to Jason and Seb order had been restored and Number 3, Bluebell Row, was, once again, home to the most beautiful tree on the street.

"Now for the pièce de résistance," I said. I reached into the box and pulled out one last item – a tree angel.

Seb looked on in awe. "She's beautiful," he said.

With her long golden hair, delicate face, sweeping ivory lace dress which had been decorated in pearls, she certainly was.

"Jason?" I said, holding her towards him.

"Me?" he asked, as if unable to believe he'd be trusted with such an honour. Jason smiled proudly as he looked around the room for something to stand on and opting for the coffee table, dragged it towards the tree. Carefully taking the angel from me, he stepped up onto the makeshift platform and stretched as high as he could to place her at the very top. Job done, he paused for a second as if enjoying the moment.

As he finally lowered himself down to ground level, we all stepped back to admire our efforts.

"Now the tree's really happy," Seb said. "And so am I."

"Me too," Jason said.

"And me," I said, astonished by how much fun I'd had.

CHAPTER 26

$\mathcal{F}$rank carried a stick in his mouth as we made our way back to Number 3, Bluebell Row. He'd found it at the start of our walk and despite much coaxing and grabbing on my part, he'd refused to let it go since.

Flat Cap Man had taken up his usual position opposite the shop. "Hello," I said, as we passed him by. I'd given up asking if he was okay. The only response I ever got was a polite confirmation that all was well before he scurried off.

"Evening," Flat Cap Man replied. He was obviously as used to seeing me as I was him by then, because gone was his fluster. Much to my surprise, he simply nodded and smiled, and stayed put, while I continued to wonder what his story was.

With Aunt Lillian's cottage in sight, I looked forward to some quiet time. Looking after Seb had been exhausting even with Jason's help. Boy, could the two of them talk. On and on, they'd wittered, chatting about anything and everything. Even when it came to Jules's activities, there was a discussion to be had thanks to Jason's bizarre ability to remember pieces of random information. When it came to the subject of Christmas, what that man didn't know clearly wasn't worth knowing.

Like the fact that a gentleman called Erwin Perzy created the very first snow globe back in 1900. Although, according to Jason this was quite by accident. The man's intention had been to improve the brightness of the newly invented electric light bulb. Then there was the brief history of the pompom that Jason had treat us to, the origins of which could be traced back to Scandinavia and the Viking era. But whereas Seb had soaked up this mine of useless information, my brain wasn't quite the sponge it once was and the second the two of them had left, I'd needed to get out into the fresh air to clear the fuzziness in my head.

I smiled as I pictured the three of us. All colouring, crafting and singing along to Christmas carols. I thought back to my own childhood recalling how mine and Mum's festivities hadn't been quite so much fun, and for the first time, I felt a little sad because of that. I appreciated why, of course. Mum was busy with two jobs and I supposed decorating the Christmas tree was just another task that needed squeezing in. Working and raising a child on her own didn't leave much time for frivolities and when she wasn't out earning, recharging her batteries had to have taken priority. No doubt, that was why she got on with tree duties when I wasn't around. I sighed. Thanks to a single afternoon with Seb and Jason, I'd had a taste of what both Mum and I had missed out on.

Nevertheless, as endearing and fun as my afternoon had been, it had also left me feeling shattered and in need of a long soak and an early night.

Frank dropped his stick at the front door, and I put it to one side, before letting us both into the house. I hung the dog's lead on the bottom of the banister and shrugged off my coat and boots, already imagining sinking into a hot deep bubble bath. I looked forward to getting into my pyjamas ready for a good night's sleep in a warm comfy bed. However, a knock at the door put a halt to my reverie and I turned, grimacing at the interruption. Frank headed into the lounge leaving me to find out who'd come a-calling. "Hello," I said, opening the door to find Oliver stood there. He held a wooden kitchen chair in his hands.

"For you," he said.

Confused by the offering, I wasn't sure how to respond.

"It's from Granddad. He said you'd know why."

I smiled as I took in the well-worn pine of the piece and recognising it from Ted Sharples's skip, I stood aside, appreciating the gesture. "Aw, that's so sweet of him," I said. "You'd better bring it in."

Oliver stepped into the hall, evidently confused. "Would you like me to put it anywhere in particular?" he said.

"No. You can just leave it here," I replied. "And, please, pass on my thanks."

"I'm to tell you there's more where this came from if you're interested."

My eyes lit up. "Really?"

Oliver laughed. "I'm not sure what this is about, but I'd have thought there was more than enough furniture here already."

"Oh, it's not for this house," I replied. "It's for my new venture."

Oliver raised an eyebrow. "Which is?"

"I can tell you over a hot chocolate?" I said. "You look as cold as I feel after being out there."

He nodded. "Why not?" He took off his coat and hung it over the bottom of the banister.

Leading the way to the kitchen, just the thought of obtaining my first acquisition had renewed my energy levels and I couldn't wait to share my plans. I set about making our drinks, all the while telling Oliver about my intention to become a roadside reclamation specialist. I rambled on about the fabulous website and Instagram account I planned on building to advertise my wares and how Jules's fixation with daytime TV had put the idea into my head. I explained that some items might only need a simple makeover, which I could manage myself, while other things would be upcycled into something new completely. Of course, that part of the business would mean subcontracting out to various craftsmen, but long term, I hoped to develop my own hands-on skills with proper training.

Oliver looked at me in the same way Jules had when I first told her my intentions – with a mix of horror and amusement. "You've decided to become a skip rat?"

"No," I replied, ready to put the man straight. "Like I said, my title is..." As I handed him his mug of hot chocolate, I clocked the twinkle in his eyes and realising he was teasing stopped short of finishing my sentence.

"Whatever you call yourself, it's a great idea," he said. "Very entrepreneurial."

I smiled at the man. It was nice to hear something positive about my intentions, for once. "Rummaging in someone else's trash isn't what many people would call fun," I said.

Oliver laughed. "Oh, I'm sure there'll be a downside to it. But imagine the rewards if you find even one bit of treasure. I'm not sure Granddad's chair will make you a fortune though."

"Oh, I don't know. After a good sand and a wax it'll hold its own," I said. "I might even paint it."

"I can keep my eye out for any renovations in the area if you like?"

"Yes, please," I replied, glad of the offer. "I wasn't planning on getting properly started until after Christmas, but I had hoped to collect a few items while I'm here, in readiness."

"New year, new start?"

"More like new year, needs must. That's why I bought Violet."

"Violet?"

"My van. In case I come across anything."

"I did wonder. Most city folks turn up in fancy cars. Range Rovers with pristine tyres, nothing like the muddied up four-by-fours the locals drive."

I giggled. I couldn't afford a swanky car even if I'd wanted one. Unlike Jules and Harry. I wondered what the locals would have made of them had they been able to make the trip. Hers and Harry's car wasn't quite the SVAutobiography, but compared to Violet, it was certainly up there. "There's nothing fancy about me, I'm afraid."

"Oh, I don't know," Oliver said, keeping his eyes firmly on mine as he put his mug to his lips and drank.

I felt myself blush and while a part of me insisted the man was simply teasing again, a part of me felt sure he wasn't. Needing the diversion, I picked up my own cup to hide behind.

"So how are you finding our little village? Have you managed to do much exploring since...?"

While glad the conversation had moved swiftly on, I continued to redden thanks to the Fotherghyll Fell reference. Despite doing my best to forget the whole incident, I kept being reminded of it.

"We could try again?" he said, tentative. "Go somewhere different?"

I looked back at the man, my face deadpan. "I take it by different, you mean flat?"

Oliver bit down on his lip and I knew he was trying not to laugh. "I do," he replied. "No hills or mountains involved."

"Around here?" I said. The man had clearly forgotten we were in the Yorkshire Dales. Besides, having embarrassed myself in front of Oliver enough times already, I wasn't sure I could risk an opportunity to do it again.

"Have a think about it," Oliver said. He put his cup down and stood up to leave. "I'm sure between us we can find something to do that we'd both enjoy."

As Oliver held my gaze, I took in his blond hair, green eyes, and gorgeous physique, while numerous fun activities flooded into my head thick and fast. I could see from the wide smile on Oliver's lips that mine wasn't the only brain going into overdrive. Lordy, even the man's teeth were perfect.

Suddenly feeling a tad warm, I, too, rose to my feet. "I'll see you out, shall I?" I said, forced to remind myself that I didn't do casual.

CHAPTER 27

Sat on the sofa, I propped my phone against the bowl on the coffee table and clicked to video call Jules. Again, I couldn't believe how calm she looked when she answered. She'd been stuck in that chair for weeks and being such an active person, I really had expected her to be struggling.

"Just a sec," she said. Holding a string of thick green cotton in one hand, she put the end between her lips to straighten it, before trying to thread the sewing needle that she held in the other. Appearing slightly cross-eyed, it took a good few tries before she managed to complete the task and watching her was painful viewing. "Finally," she said.

"What are you up to now?" I asked. Having seen Jules's attempt at knitting, I dreaded to think.

She held up a piece of aida, secured in a couple of bamboo embroidery hoops. "Cross-stitch," she said.

"Another Christmas gift?" I asked, wondering who the lucky recipient could be.

"Yep." She picked up a piece of paper for me to see. "What do you think?"

Assuming I was looking at the pattern she had followed, I

found myself forced to squint as I tried to decipher what I was looking at. Consisting of a grid covered in tiny symbols, no way could I make the image out.

"It's holly and ivy," Jules said, studying the design for a second. "It's playing havoc with my eyes." She put her latest project to one side, at last, giving me her full attention. She frowned. "Speaking of not being able to see, why is it so dark where you are?"

I picked up my phone and directed the camera towards the Christmas tree in the window.

"Wow!" she said.

"Tell me about it."

"That's a bit different to your usual effort." Jules suddenly froze. "Does this mean you're doing the Christmas swap?" She let out a squeal as she put a hand up to her mouth in anticipation of my answer.

I wrinkled my nose and realising how things must have looked, my gaze went from Jules to the tree and back again. "I haven't decided," I said. Despite having no intention of taking part, I couldn't bring myself to let her down completely. "I'm still thinking about it."

"But I've put together a menu for you, complete with shopping list and I've..." Her good mood seemed to wane.

"The tree was a present," I said, cheerful. Hoping to divert her attention, I was reluctant to say who from. Jules needed to find out for herself that Jason wasn't quite the individual she remembered. "A couple of locals dropped it round."

As usual, Jules wasn't for giving up. "Well you better start thinking harder. Christmas Day's only a week off."

Didn't I know it. I'd landed in Little Leatherington with such good intentions. However, when it came to sorting out my new role, thanks to numerous interruptions, my head hadn't always been in the game and productivity had been lacking. "I will," I said, ready to talk about something else.

Jules sighed. "It was very thoughtful of them, though. Didn't I tell you the place wasn't filled with weirdos? That they're just people wanting to welcome a newcomer?"

I'd yet to completely come round to that way of thinking.

"I mean that's some gift."

I stared at the branches before me, taking in the travelling Father Christmas, the silver bell baubles and the porcelain candy canes. "Lillian's tree ornaments are fabulous, Jules. You're going to love them. Seb certainly had a great time hanging everything."

"So the babysitting was a success?" Jules asked.

As she, at last, livened up at little, I had to wonder if Jules wasn't as happy as she had seemed. "Thanks to you," I said, picturing Seb, crayon in hand, putting the festive stencils to good use. "Those activities you sent through were brilliant. They really did keep him entertained."

"Glad to be of assistance," Jules said. She raised her eyebrows. "Any other news you'd like to share?"

I knew what she was getting at. "If you're talking about Oliver..."

"Who else?"

I steeled myself. "He's asked me out."

Jules let out another squeal and bounced up and down in her seat. "When? Where? How?"

"I'm not going."

Jules's bouncing stopped. She stared at me. "Why not?"

"Because if I spend more than five minutes with the man, I end up looking like a fool." I pictured myself halfway up Fotherghyll Fell, mascara down my cheeks as I clung to its rock face. I recalled standing there, poker in hand, ready to fight off a bovine named Clarabelle, and I remembered how I'd lectured

Oliver for giving me dirty looks, after telling him to show his own grandfather some respect.

Jules tried to stifle her laugh. "Please don't tell me there's more." Despite her protest, I could see she secretly hoped I would.

I told her about the night in the pub. About how I'd accused Oliver of glaring at me, except he hadn't been focusing on me at all; his attention had been on Ted.

"So, the grumpy old man is his granddad?" Jules asked, her eyes wide. "Well, I didn't see that coming."

"It came as a surprise to me, too," I replied, squirming at my behaviour.

"Oliver couldn't have been bothered by what you said, though. Otherwise, he wouldn't have asked you out."

"I suppose," I said, thinking Jules had a point.

"And while you're not looking for a relationship, it wouldn't hurt to have some fun," she said. "If I were you, I'd be jumping at the chance to spend a few hours with a man like that. He's gorgeous."

I laughed. "I wouldn't let Harry hear you say that." My brow furrowed as I realised what Jules had just said. "Hang on. You've seen him?"

"I checked out his profile on his company website."

I shook my head. Of course, she did. It was just like Jules to do something like that.

"So where does he plan on taking you?"

"I don't know. To check out a few good skips, maybe."

Jules's draw dropped. "You haven't told him you've decided to become a skip rat?"

"Roadside reclamation specialist, if you don't mind."

"And the man still asked you out?" Trying to keep a straight face, Jules bit down on her lips.

I came over all smug. "For your information, he thinks it's a great idea. He called me an entrepreneur."

"Very forward thinking," Jules said, laughing. She suddenly turned serious. "Oh, Antonia, you have to go out with him. The man sounds like an absolute catch."

I scoffed. "Why? Because he complimented my new job? Jules, you know how these things go. One minute what I do is fantastic, and sixty seconds later they sound like you. Telling me I should get a proper job. Besides, I'm not looking for a catch."

"Maybe not. But you deserve some fun, at least. Come on, it's Christmas. Let your hair down for once." She suddenly straightened herself up, excitement written all over her face. "Antonia, if all goes well you could invite him for Christmas dinner. And Ted. Oh, I bet the old man would love that."

"What are you talking about now?"

"Our Christmas swap."

A high-pitched shrill rang out from the side of Jules's chair. She reached down and picked up some gadget – an alarm – that she proceeded to switch off.

"What's that for?" I asked.

"There's something I want to watch on TV. This is my reminder that it's about to start. It's a show about interior design. If there's one thing I've realised sitting here looking at these four walls for weeks on end, it's that we're due a revamp. I'm hoping to pick up some tips."

I chuckled. The poor woman really needed to get that cast off so she could start living a normal life again. "I'll let you get going then, shall I?"

"Yes, please," Jules replied. "But promise you'll call Oliver. That you'll go out on that date."

I opened my mouth to speak, but my friend interrupted.

"I know what you're going to say," she said. "But telling me you'll think about that too, isn't an option."

I couldn't help but smile as we ended the call. From card-making to knitting to cross-stitch and more, my friend seemed to be making the most out of her confinement. Although as I continued to consider her predicament, my heart went out to Jules. I supposed it was no wonder she got frustrated with me. Despite her enthusiasm for all things crafting, she probably wanted nothing more than to get out of the house. Yet there I was, choosing to be stuck indoors when I didn't have to be.

I chewed on the inside of my cheek, as I considered my friend's advice. No way was I inviting Oliver for Christmas, but I supposed a date wouldn't do any harm. For Jules's sake, if not mine. Picking up my phone, I searched for Oliver's number, ready to start keying in a text. "I'm doing this for you, Jules," I said, as I began to type. Message written, I clicked send.

CHAPTER 28

Telling myself I had better things to do than keep checking my phone to see if Oliver had replied, I decided to get on with some research. I still hadn't found a reasonably priced storage and workshop facility ready for the new year; something I desperately needed for my venture to succeed. I grabbed my laptop off the sideboard, switched it on and signed in. But as I was about to hit the internet to try yet another search, a knock at the door interrupted me. My shoulders dropped. "Why am I not surprised?" I said.

Frank looked up from his prone position in front of the fire. Watching him put his head back down, I couldn't believe how lazy he'd become since we'd landed in Little Leatherington. The only time he seemed to run anywhere of late was in his dreams.

Leaving him to it, I got up and went to answer, opening the door to find Lizzie and Seb waiting to greet me.

"We made you these," Seb said. Standing proud, he held out a Tupperware tub for me to take. "Christmas cookies."

"To say thank you for yesterday," Lizzie said. "I don't know when I'd have got my shopping done if you hadn't looked after this one." She ruffled the top of her son's head.

I opened the plastic tub to see it packed with star-shaped biscuits, each covered in white icing and multicoloured sprinkles. "And very nice they look too," I said to Seb, who puffed his chest out all the more.

"They taste good as well," the little boy said.

I smiled. "You know what would go perfectly with these?" I asked.

Seb shook his head.

"Hot chocolate." I turned my attention to Lizzie. "Fancy joining me?"

"Only if you're not busy," she replied.

Despite having a tonne of research to get on with, I thought about Jules, stuck in her chair, cut off from all human contact, apart from Harry. "Not at all," I said. I stood aside for them to enter and while Seb headed straight for the lounge to see Frank, Lizzie followed me down the hall to the kitchen. I put the Tupperware down on the counter and began heating up the milk for our drinks. "So are you ready for Christmas now, then?" I asked.

"Thanks to you, I'm almost there," Lizzie replied. "I've still got a couple of bits to pick up, but I'm not panicking. What about you? All organised?"

"I'd say so. With just me to think about, there isn't much to do. As long as I have enough food in, so I don't starve, that's the main thing." With the hot chocolate made, I handed Lizzie her cup and we headed through to join Seb.

Frank was on his back, with his tongue hanging out to one side, as Seb rubbed his tummy. "Can we get a dog, Mummy?" the little boy asked.

Lizzie scoffed. "That would be a no," she replied.

"Why not?"

"Because I have enough to think about looking after you."

Seb laughed. "You are funny, Mummy."

Lizzie's mobile began to ring and pulling it out of her jeans pocket a little smile crossed her lips. "Do you mind if I take this?" she asked, already rising.

"Of course not," I said. Watching her hastily head out into the hall, I heard the front door open and close. Whatever the call was about, she definitely wanted to keep it private. Why else would she have gone out into the cold?

"It'll be Barrowboy," Seb said. "I'm not supposed to know. Mum's trying to protect me. She thinks I'll worry if she meets someone new. But Daddy's got a special friend, so why shouldn't Mummy have one too?" He wrinkled his nose. "At least, that's what I think."

I smiled. At only seven years old, Seb seemed to be an insightful little boy.

He stopped stroking Frank to look at me, pensive. "That's not all that's bothering her though."

"What do you mean?" I asked. Seeing his concern, I wondered where his conversation was going.

Seb sighed. "She's worried about Christmas. It's our first without Daddy. It'll be just the two of us. And I know she doesn't have much money. Not like before, when Daddy lived with us. I think that's why she does a lot of sums."

I recalled my own childhood, remembering how hard it was for my mum to balance the books. As if making the money coming in stretch wasn't difficult enough, Christmas only added to the pressure. I could still see the sadness on her face when I opened my presents because she hadn't been able to afford much. She never meant for me to see her pain, of course. But it was there, behind her smile. As far back as I could remember I understood why that would hurt. While everyone at school seemed to be inundated with the latest brands, crazes, and technology, my presents didn't compete. And boy did the other kids let me know it. Except for Jules. My one and only friend in the world, she didn't tease. Although looking back, teasing didn't seem the right word. Bullying was more like it. I didn't care that they laughed at me, though. Mum's lack of money made every present she bought me even more special. Year upon year, I prized every gift she gave me and listening to Seb, I was sure he would too when it came to Lizzie.

"Why are there no presents under your tree?" Seb asked. He rose and began searching under its lower branches.

"Santa doesn't come for almost a week," I replied.

"But what about from people you know?" The little boy's brow furrowed. "Don't you have any friends?"

I did my best not to smile. "Of course, I do," I said, trying to reassure him. "But they live in London."

He looked at me, aghast. "So you'll be on your own on Christmas Day?"

"I will."

"But you can't be. How will you celebrate?" He stared at me like I was weird. "A party of one is not a celebration." Listening to him, he was beginning to sound like Jules.

"It is for me," I said. "I like my own company. I get to laze around in my pyjamas and eat what I want when I want. And I can watch telly or read a book without being disturbed."

He suddenly looked sad. "I bet you're only saying that."

"I'm not. Besides, I have Frank to keep me company."

"But he's a dog." The little boy swallowed, as if he was about to cry. "He doesn't count."

I felt my heart melt at Seb's concern. He looked so innocent, standing there willing his tears away. "Honestly, Seb. I'll be absolutely fine."

He seemed to think for a moment, before suddenly wiping his eyes and pulling himself together. "Don't worry, Antonia. I have a plan."

"A plan?" I asked.

"Yes. Everyone can stop worrying. I'm going to tell Mummy we don't have to be on our own on Christmas Day because we're coming here, to spend it with you."

"Sweetheart, no. Really, that's not necessary."

"Well I think it is."

"Everything all right?" Lizzie asked. Appearing in the doorway, she looked from Seb to me. "Anything I should know about?"

Seb jumped to his feet, ready to outline his proposal. "Mummy, you know how you keep telling me Christmas is a time to give?" He was so determined that his plan was put into action he talked with his hands throughout. "Which is why we put those shoe boxes with crayons and drawing books and toothbrushes together?"

"Yes," his mum replied, her voice cautious as if wondering what was coming next.

"Well, we need to give to Antonia."

"It's very kind of you to think that way, Seb, but..."

"Look," he said to his mum, before I could finish. He pointed to the Christmas tree. "She has no presents because she doesn't have any friends."

"Seb, my friends are in London, remember. That's where I live."

"And she's spending Christmas all on her own," he carried on, as if I hadn't spoken. "So we'll have to come here for the day. So she isn't sad and lonely. Like you."

That wasn't quite the description I would have given myself and going off Lizzie's shocked expression, she wouldn't have described herself that way either.

Lizzie stood there, clearly as embarrassed as I was.

"Please, Mummy," he said. "We have to." A tear rolled down the little boy's cheek. "Antonia can't spend Christmas on her own. That wouldn't be fair. She just can't." He raced over to his mum, threw his arms around her waist and buried his head in her tummy.

As Seb began to sob, Lizzie tried to comfort him. She looked my way, as surprised as me by her son's outburst. Her expression was desperate, but neither of us knew what to say.

Taking in the little boy's anguish, I guessed he was the one worried about his dad not being there that year, not Lizzie as he'd claimed, and seeing him so confused and upset was heartbreaking. Not celebrating with both parents had to be difficult to get his young head around. Seb was evidently a sensitive little boy underneath, despite his, at times, confident demeanour, and I felt his pain, as I readily pictured him sat there wearing a sad face on Christmas morning because rather than think of himself, he'd be too busy thinking about his dad, or about me for being on my own. "You're both more than welcome to spend the day with me," I said, for my sake as much as Seb's. "If you want to."

Seb lifted his head, his face red and distraught. "Really?"

I smiled a gentle smile and nodded.

"Mummy, can we?" Seb asked, his tear-stained face full of anticipation.

Lizzie again looked my way. I could see she was torn between appeasing her son and not wanting to impose.

"It's all right with me," I said, wanting to reassure Lizzie. "If it's all right with you."

She sighed, as if glad the choice had been made for her. "Thank you," she said. "We'd love to come."

Seb jumped up and down. "Did you hear that, Frank? We're spending Christmas with you and Antonia." He raced over to the dog and hugged him tight.

Lizzie and I looked at each other. "I'm sorry," Lizzie said.

"Don't be," I replied, as my phone bleeped indicating a text had come through.

CHAPTER 29

*I*t still wasn't properly light as I led Frank down Little Leatherington's main street. I hadn't slept very well following Seb's emotional outburst. He'd been through a lot of changes in the previous twelve months and his little brain was obviously still trying to get to grips with the impact of his parents' divorce and as a result of seeing him like that, I'd spent the night more catnapping than anything. In the end I'd become so frustrated at not being able to properly drop off, I'd climbed out of bed, thrown on the day before's clothes, and headed out into the dawn air.

As I trudged along with sleep in my eyes, I had to wonder what I'd been thinking when I'd succumbed to Seb's request. Having never hosted a Christmas lunch before, I didn't have a clue where to start. I wasn't a complete numpty in the kitchen, but I doubted cooking for three was the same as cooking for one; especially when, in my experience, cooking for one usually involved a microwave.

Never in my life had I oven-roasted a whole turkey, let alone had to bring multiple timings into the mix thanks to everything else that went on the plate. As Frank and I made our way back to

Number 3, Bluebell Row, I knew the best chance I had if I wanted to anywhere near succeed, was to get Jules on the case. Calling her, however, would have to wait and not just because of the ungodly hour. First, I had to get my date with Oliver out of the way so I could focus; another reason why I'd spent most of the night tossing and turning. Wondering why I'd agreed to that too, I tried to ignore the butterflies in my tummy. I had so much to do in the run up to Christmas Day, with less than a week to go, my time could have been better spent.

At last, the sun began to show itself, causing the hard frost that had settled in the surrounding fields to glimmer and shine. Sheep lay chest down, with their heads resting on the cold ground in front of them. And there was a mist in the distance, while winter birds heralded the new day.

Letting myself and Frank into the house, I headed straight for the kitchen. Clicking the kettle on, I stared out into the garden while I waited for it to boil. The sun shone in the increasingly blue sky, brightening up the whole space. "At least we have the weather for it," I said to Frank, of my date with Oliver.

As I made my drink, he nudged his bowl my way with his nose, showing me he had other priorities. I scoffed and picking it up to feed him, wished that filling my belly was all I had to think about.

While Frank ate his breakfast, I drank my coffee, then headed back upstairs to get showered and dressed. I didn't have a clue what Oliver had planned for the day. Although when it came to my attire, it didn't really matter. Having expected to spend my time in Little Leatherington dog walking and not much else, dress code or not, I already knew my clothing options were limited. I opened the wardrobe in my room and stared at the rail. Rifling along the hangers it appeared I had jeans, jeans and yet more jeans, along with a sweater, another sweater and yet more sweaters. I could already see Jules shaking her head if I even dared wear such an ensemble for a date.

I plonked myself down on the bed, feeling annoyed. Partly because I hadn't come prepared for all eventualities and partly because my failure seemed to matter. I wondered what was wrong with me. Yes, there were times when I needed to play dress-up. But I had to ask if meandering around the Yorkshire Dales in the middle of winter was really one of them? I sighed. As much as I wanted to deny it, on that occasion it was. I took another deep breath and exhaled again, wondering what to do.

"Unless..." I looked towards the door and the landing beyond, realising I did, in fact, have another option.

I'd styled my hair into a messy chignon, put on a bit of mascara and lip gloss, and, as I swept my way downstairs, had the air of a movie star.

Initially, I'd felt uncomfortable as I rummaged through the black bin bags containing Aunt Lillian's clothes. Like a looter, or one of the vagabonds who stole Ebenezer Scrooge's belongings as he lay on his deathbed in *A Christmas Carol*. But trying on glamorous item after glamorous item, I soon got lost in the fun of it. Talk about a mood lifter; there had been so much to choose from.

In the end, I'd opted for a 1950s raglan blouse, made out of cool, crisp cotton. Navy blue in colour, it had cuffed three-quarter length sleeves, with four contrasting huge white buttons running down the front. Its collar came down towards the chest in a lapelled fashion and it teamed perfectly with a pair of my own skinny jeans and borrowed grey woollen trench coat. I looked down at my feet. Even my trusty Doc Martens looked great. "What do you think, Frank?" I asked. Heading into the lounge, I gave him a twirl.

I stopped still thanks to a knock at the door and my heart skipped a beat. This was the first date I'd been on in a year and despite not expecting anything to come of it, I still felt nervous. "You be good," I said to Frank, who'd snuggled himself up on the sofa. I grabbed my bag and exited into the hall, pausing to take a deep breath. I glanced down at my attire to give it a final once-over, before opening the door to greet Oliver.

He wore a white Oxford button-down shirt, a textured blazer, and wool chinos. Finished off with a pair of brown brogues, he looked smart yet casual and I thanked goodness I hadn't simply thrown on a jumper. "Ready to go?" he asked.

I nodded and, stepping outside, closed the front door behind me.

"You look nice," he said.

Taking in his appreciative smile, butterflies once again played havoc in my tummy. "Thank you," I replied. Happy to accept the compliment, I didn't have the heart to tell him half my outfit belonged to a dead woman.

CHAPTER 30

I took in our surroundings as we drove along country roads and passed through villages. Despite the sunshine and blue skies, frost glistened on cottage roofs and smoke billowed from chimneys, showing just how cold the day's temperature was. As I stared out of the window, a little voice insisted I had more important things to do than ride around the countryside. But refusing to listen, I pushed all thoughts of the next few days to the back of my mind, knowing I'd soon enough be run ragged trying to get ready for Christmas.

I didn't have a clue where we were headed. Oliver had refused to divulge. "So where did you say we're going?" Making sure to sound casual, I snuck a glance his way, hoping Oliver would forget himself and let slip our destination.

A smile crossed his lips, but he kept his eyes on the road. "I didn't," he replied. "I said it was a surprise."

"And if I don't like surprises?" I said.

"Not an issue. You'll love this one."

Admiring the man's confidence, I realised there was no point trying to guess. We could have been going anywhere. According to Jules's research there were lots of events in the area. From bandstand carol concerts to pop-up ice rinks and everything in between. I just hoped we weren't about to partake in the latter. I struggled to stay upright in a pair of boots thanks to the freezing weather, no way could I have managed on blades. I pictured myself on an icy arena, flailing my arms around as I slipped and slid because my feet refused to co-ordinate. Shaking the image away, I knew I'd spend more time on my backside than I would any vertical position and as far as I was concerned, I'd embarrassed myself enough in front of Oliver Chase.

"Granddad said to say hello," Oliver said.

I smiled. "How is he?"

"Grumpy as ever."

I let out a laugh as I pictured Ted, sat with his arms folded, with a cranky look on his face. "I wouldn't expect anything else."

"He said to remind you to come and have a nosey in his skip. Although to be honest, I doubt there's much in there worth salvaging."

"You never know. The little chair he gave me doesn't need much TLC."

"I think he just wants to see you again. He likes your company." Oliver turned his head to look at me. "He's not the only one."

He held my gaze for a moment longer than necessary, and I felt myself blush thanks to the intenseness in his eyes. And while he returned his attention to the road with another little smile, I tried to quell the fuzziness in my tummy.

"You need to stop doing that," I said.

"Doing what?"

"Looking at me as if you're... you know? Attracted to me."

Oliver flicked on the car's indicator, before pulling over to the left and bringing the car to a standstill.

"What are you doing?" I asked, suddenly confused.

He took off his seat belt and unclipped mine. Without saying a word, he got out of the vehicle altogether and walked round to the passenger side.

"Where are we going?" I couldn't see anything but fields.

Opening my door, he took my hand and pulled me onto my feet. My heart raced as he gently cupped my face in his hands, all the while keeping his eyes on mine. He seemed to be about to kiss me. Jesus, in that moment I wanted him to kiss me.

"May I?" he asked.

My brain screamed *no!* It told me I was going back to London in just over a week and that I needed to be sensible. It reminded me that I didn't do casual or partake in holiday romances. It insisted I had more important things to think about than Oliver Chase. Like organising Christmas and sorting out my new venture.

My head, however, nodded.

Slowly, he brought his lips closer to mine, until at last they touched in the gentlest and sweetest of caresses. My body began to melt as one caress led to another and then another. Our lips parted, and our tongues entwined. I heard myself moan. Oliver's kiss tasted so good, I wanted it to go on forever.

He pulled away. "Antonia," he said, his tone soft. "I look at you the way I do sometimes because I'm *more* than attracted to you."

I swallowed, hard. "That's not the point," I said.

Oliver laughed. "You know you're as weird as the rest of us around here, right?" He stood back and gestured to the car and, thinking that was the most romantic experience I'd ever had, I climbed in while he made his way back round to the driver's side.

"I've wanted to do that since I very first saw you, by the way."

As we continued on our journey, no way was I admitting I'd felt the same about him.

"Speaking of odd characters," I said, instead. "What's the

story with the chap outside the shop?" While I seemed to be getting an angle on most of the people I'd come across, I'd yet to understand Flat Cap Man. "You must have seen him? Smart appearance, drives an old car?"

"You're talking about Lewis. The local landowner."

Thinking about it, he did look quite the squire.

"He has a thing for Marianne, the shopkeeper."

I frowned. "Why doesn't he just tell her? Explain how he feels?"

He raised an eyebrow. "Why not, indeed?"

I gave him a playful tap on the arm.

"It's not that he hasn't tried, but Lewis isn't the most confident of individuals. Every time he goes in, she never looks up from her book long enough to notice him, so he bottles it, buys the first thing to hand and leaves."

"So all that pacing up and down is him trying to pluck up the courage to ask her out?"

"It is."

"The poor man."

"He'll get there," Oliver said.

Picturing Lewis's desperation as he strode back and forth, I couldn't say I shared Oliver's optimism.

Oliver turned to face me. "We're not really as mad as we seem, you know. I get that you probably think us a weird bunch, but stay long enough, and you'll find we're actually quite normal. Plus, we accept people for who they are." He smiled. "Even skip rats."

I let out a laugh. "Roadside reclamation specialist," I replied, correcting him.

He smiled. "Those too." He faced the road again. "Seriously, people in Little Leatherington are hard-working. They don't always have time for niceties, they're too busy trying to earn a living. Most of us come from farming stock, and believe me, that way of life isn't easy. Look at Barrowboy. He runs his place more or less single-handed. I can't remember when he last had a day off."

"If I didn't know any better, I'd say you're trying to get me to stay."

He looked at me direct again. "Would that be a bad thing?"

I felt my cheeks redden, while he got back to his driving.

"Here we are," Oliver said, in a change of subject. He flicked on the car's indicator for a second time, before slowing the vehicle and making his turn.

Wondering where we were, my curiosity grew. I scanned the area as we drove down a long, sweeping, tree-lined drive, straightening up in my seat as a huge English country mansion came into view. Built from yellow limestone, it stood proud, three floors high, against the blue sky, four central pillars heralding its grand entranceway.

"Welcome to Missingham House," Oliver said, a big grin on his face.

"What are we doing here?" I asked.

The man's refusal to give anything away continued. "You'll see."

I couldn't wait to find out and unclipping my seat belt in readiness, I absorbed the grandness around me. I thanked goodness I'd made an effort on the attire front, at the same time wondering if we were about to enjoy a festive afternoon tea in the house's – no doubt posh – dining room. I might not have been a fan of cucumber sandwiches and Christmas cake, but I did love a good Victoria sponge. I readily envisaged myself drinking from a vintage floral cup and saucer, my little finger protruding accordingly.

My excitement grew as Oliver manoeuvred the car towards the car park off to the side of the building. Looking at the number of vehicles around us, Missingham House was evidently popular and as we disembarked, I began walking back towards the front of the property.

"It's this way," Oliver said, indicating we were headed around the back.

"Oh, okay," I replied. Forced to ignore the chink in my enthusiasm, I followed in Oliver's footsteps as we made our way round to the tradesman's entrance.

CHAPTER 31

I felt Oliver slip his palm in mine as we followed the line of a tall red-brick wall that led round to the back of the building. Usually when a man did that, I'd pull away. But with Oliver, I didn't feel the need. Holding his hand as we walked felt natural. Right, even.

He drew me to a standstill when we reached a two-storey folly that sat mid-point in the wall's rear aspect. It had a wide archway cut through it, signalling what looked like the only entrance into what I assumed would be a courtyard.

"After you," Oliver said, with a wide grin on his face.

As we stepped through, my eyes widened. Not only was I right about there being an enclosure it was vast, consisting of a huge circular lawn surrounded by a wide gravel path. Outbuildings sat both left and right. With their glass roofs, I deemed them far too grand to be stables or workshops. "This is gorgeous," I said. I couldn't wait to find out what we were doing there.

The house's rear entrance might have had a bigger than average doorway, but it was nowhere near as spectacular as the one at the front. However, if what I'd seen so far was anything to go by, I knew what lay behind it had to be magnificent.

"You ready?" Oliver asked, ready to enter.

"I certainly am," I replied, giggling. I continued to beam as he swung the door open, but as we crossed the threshold, my smile froze. There was no splendour before us, just a wide whitewashed corridor reminiscent of those found in a Victorian hospital. I turned to Oliver, hoping he'd tell me we'd taken a wrong turn. But he didn't seem fazed.

"This is going to be so much fun," he said, instead.

A woman, wearing a welcoming smile and brightly coloured elf costume, appeared at the far end of the passage. "Would you like to come this way, please," she said, indicating we follow her.

Taking in her green dress with its red star collar and matching hat, I wondered what Santa's little helper could possibly want with us. More to the point, what Oliver had got me into. But as I, again, looked to him for an explanation, he simply chuckled, his lips remaining sealed on that front.

"Don't worry," he said, nudging me forward. "You're going to love it."

Shaking my head at the woman's red and green striped tights and felted boots, I doubted that very much.

Elf woman directed us into a room full of people and as mums, dads, and their children all clamoured over each other trying to be heard, the resulting noise bounced off the walls. Colouring books and felt-tip pens sat on tables for the younger attendees and a box of toys had been placed in the corner. As I continued to glance around, my confusion reigned.

A male member of Santa's entourage came to the door. "Danny Malone," he called out.

A little boy raised his hand, stretching his arm as high as he could.

"Would you like to come this way?"

The boy jumped to his feet and headed for the door, leaving his parents no choice but to hasten after him and again, I looked to Oliver. However, he simply smiled and shrugged in response.

"Oliver Chase," Elf woman said, reappearing in the doorway.

"Here!" Oliver replied. Hand up, he certainly gave Danny Malone a run for his money.

The woman gestured us forward. "This way, please."

Oliver guided me back out into the corridor but as we followed the woman around the corner, our route didn't seem to go anywhere. There were no doors leading off the passageway, just a huge wardrobe at the far end. My bewilderment grew as the three of us approached the strangely placed hunk of furniture.

Elf woman opened the wardrobe doors to reveal a line of thick fur coats.

I looked from her to Oliver, wondering if I was supposed to put one on.

"In you go," the woman said, gesturing for me to climb in.

I scoffed. "Where are we off to? Narnia?"

Oliver nodded, also indicating I get in. "Time to find out," he said.

With nothing else for it, I decided to play along, and with Oliver close behind, I pushed the coats out of the way and made my way through. My eyes widened as I stepped out of the other side. "It's like we're in another world," I said, struggling to believe what I was seeing.

"Didn't I tell you you'd love it," Oliver said.

I stared at the giant fir trees surrounding me, the Christmas trolls peeking out from their hiding places, and the fake snow covering the ground. Blue lighting created a real Winter Wonderland feel. I stretched up and kissed Oliver's cheek. "And you were right," I said.

Thrown back to when I was young, I recalled all the library

visits mum and I had made. Books took me to imaginary places inhabited by the most wonderful of characters. I'd have lived amongst those library shelves if I could. Sometimes mum would read the stories to me, but mostly I'd lose myself in page after page of enchanted fairy tales. Glancing around this place, it was as if I'd landed in one of my childhood reads.

Oliver took my hand in his and as we began walking, I couldn't stop smiling. We followed the path through the forest, until we came to another door. "What now?" I asked, intrigued.

"We knock," Oliver said.

He rapped hard on the wood and after a moment the door slowly opened as if by itself and, leaving the trees behind, we entered the most opulent room I'd ever seen. Large traditional tapestry rugs covered its old wooden floor and while rich timber panelling adorned its lower walls, numerous old paintings and portraits hung above. Raising my gaze, I couldn't help but admire the original plaster cornicing that framed the ceiling, and I marvelled at the enormous ornate chandelier that lit up the room from a carved central rose. "This is beautiful," I said.

My gaze turned to the open fire that danced in an Adam style fireplace. A high-backed armchair with a side table positioned next to it faced the flames and being so wrapped up in the grandeur of the room, it took me a moment to realise a figure was seated enjoying the warmth. I turned to Oliver, hoping that wasn't who I thought it was. "Please tell me that's not..."

"Father Christmas?" Oliver said, interrupting. "Oh, yes." His smile grew, as if a pretend Santa's presence was a good thing.

The seated figure rose to his feet. "It seems I have visitors," he said. His voice boomed. He was taking his role very seriously.

I couldn't deny he looked every bit the part. He was tall and well-built, and a wreath made from berries, leaves and twigs sat on his head of thick white hair. His beard, also pure white, reached his chest, and he wore a long grey coat just like the travelling Santa that hung from the tree at Number 3, Bluebell Row. Under that, I saw a golden tunic, while his red trousers were tucked into black boots. If I didn't know any better, I'd have sworn I was looking at the real thing.

Santa threw his arms out. "Merry Christmas," he said, his voice bellowing again. "Come." He turned the armchair round, while Oliver rummaged in his pocket and produced his mobile phone.

I looked from Oliver to Santa Claus, my eyes widening in horror as the latter sat down and tapped his knee. Surely no one really expected me to take part in a photo opportunity.

Oliver held up his camera in readiness, while I looked from one man to the other once more. Taking in their expectant expressions it seemed, yes, they blooming well did.

CHAPTER 32

I felt guilty for leaving Frank home alone all afternoon, so after changing out of Aunt Lillian's clothes and getting the open fire burning ready for a relaxed evening ahead, I eased my conscience by taking the dog on a longer than usual walk.

As we meandered through the village, stopping and starting thanks to Frank's nasal curiosity, thoughts of that afternoon swirled through my head. Missingham House had been impressive. It was grand and beautiful and, with its very own Winter Wonderland, had taken me to another world. And while the less said the better about me sitting on Santa's knee, most wonderful of all was Oliver's kiss. I could still feel the softness of his lips caressing mine. I smiled and feeling happy, warm and fuzzy I could have hugged myself. My afternoon with Oliver had been the most romantic few hours I'd ever experienced, and on so many levels.

Frank's lead suddenly snapped tight, bringing me to an immediate standstill. I turned to see the dog scratting at a wooden gate that led into a small field. A sign told me the path running up the side of the stretch of grass was a right of way and that walkers should close both entry and exit ways behind them. Wondering if I should let Frank follow his nose a while longer, my eyes scanned the area beyond. With no people, sheep or other animals in sight, I thought it only fair the dog had some fun too. Letting us in, I did as instructed and shut the gate safe and secure behind us.

Unleashing Frank altogether, he surprised me by setting off on a run and seeing him race around the field as fast as his stumpy legs would allow, it was as if I had the old Frank back. I chuckled as I watched him swerve this way and that, knowing that if he wasn't careful, he wouldn't be able to stop. I smiled at his antics, before calling out to him. "Slow down, you could get hurt," I said. My words suddenly resonated, leaving me unsure as to who needed that advice more. The dog or me?

Finally, I put Frank back on his lead. He'd found yet another stick that he just had to have, and it seemed no matter how many times I tried to relieve him of it, he was going to carry it back to Number 3. Reaching the house and unlocking the door, I shook my head as the dog dropped his latest addition onto the pile that he'd already collected. "You really are one strange hound," I said.

Stepping inside, we headed straight for the kitchen. I filled Frank's bowl with water, but he didn't drink for long. The poor dog was shattered following his extended exercise and after a few slurps, he trotted off into the lounge to, no doubt, plonk himself in front of the fire. I set about making myself a hot drink and just as I'd finished, my phone suddenly sounded. I pulled it out of my pocket and checked the screen. Smiling to myself, I took both my mobile and drink with me into the lounge.

Settling myself down on the sofa, I inhaled deeply as I clicked the answer button, readying myself for the onslaught of questions.

"Where have you been?" Jules asked, as her face appeared on screen. "I've been trying to get through for ages."

"I'm sorry," I said. Chuckling at her impatience, I could imagine the number of missed calls that would flash up once we finished talking. "I was going to ring. But Frank's been stuck in all day and needed to get out."

"I've been on pins thinking about you and Oliver," Jules said. "Wondering how things were going. There was no point me even trying to get on with my jigsaw." She flipped her camera to show me hundreds of unconnected puzzle pieces scattered over a huge board that balanced on her lap. "See!"

Once of a day, such a sight would have surprised me, but after all the crafting Jules had partaken in of late, I had to admit progressing onto jigsaws felt scarily inevitable.

"We could have talked while you walked," Jules carried on, her face reappearing. "How is the little munchkin, by the way?"

I directed my screen at Frank so she could see him lazing in front of the flames. "Comfortable," I said. "It's his favourite spot in the house."

"I can see why," Jules replied. "That fire. I'm so jealous of you both right now."

I turned the phone back on myself. "You wouldn't say that if you were the one cleaning it. Soot gets everywhere," I said. "Something you'll find out for yourself once you're up and moving again."

Jules dismissed my train of thought with a wave of her hand. "Enough about that," she said. "I'm more interested in your date with you know who." She shuffled in her seat, straightening herself up. "Tell me. How did it go?"

I smiled, at the same time feeling a tad embarrassed. "Very well actually."

"Really?" Jules said, her jaw dropping.

"Do you have to look so shocked?" I asked, laughing. "You could at least *try* and hide your amazement."

"Sorry," Jules said. "It's just you usually end your dates with a list of complaints." She reached down for her flask and poured herself a drink, before making a show of getting comfortable. "Right. I want to know everything," she said, excited. "And I mean *everything*."

As I began to divulge, it felt like we were teenagers again. Dissecting events and words to make sure no statement or signal had been misread. And just like in the good old days, Jules was more than happy to give her opinion.

"Good thinking," she said, when I told her I'd had to raid her aunt's clothing. "Although I might've been tempted to wash them first."

"That's so special," she said, almost swooning when I described how we'd climbed through a wardrobe into a magical winter wonderland.

"You sat on Santa's knee?" she asked, incredulous, when I explained where the enchanted forest had led us. "I'll need photographic evidence."

"He was suggesting what?" she asked, as if ready to have a heart attack when I said Oliver had hinted at me staying on a while longer.

Taking in her response, no way was I telling her about our kiss.

"Oh, Antonia," she said. "I think that's a great idea."

"Excuse me?" I replied, forced to wonder what the woman was thinking.

"Well, you don't have anything keeping you here." She took a sip of her drink. "Present company excepted, of course."

"Jules, my whole life's in London. My flat, my job."

"What job?"

"And in case you've forgotten." I gestured to the window

somewhere behind the Christmas tree. "This is the countryside. I hate the blooming countryside."

Jules nearly spat out her coffee. "You seem to be coping all right to me." She wiped her mouth. "Besides, these things are as hard or as easy as you want them to be."

"Anyway," I said, more than ready to move the conversation on. "I have more important things on my mind right now."

"More important than Oliver Chase?"

"Yes."

"Like what?" Jules clearly didn't agree.

"Like the fact that I'm going to need that Christmas Day menu you talked about. And the shopping list."

Jules scoffed. "Why? Don't they do microwave meals up there in the north?"

I ignored her quip. "Because I'm organising a proper Christmas dinner."

Not for the first time during our catch-up, Jules looked at me aghast.

"I have guests coming," I said. "So my usual fare won't cut it."

With her cup halfway to her mouth, Jules froze. "You have what?"

"You heard me. Guests."

"Does this mean...?"

I could see she hardly dare finish her sentence.

"I'm agreeing to your Christmas swap? Yes, it does."

"Oh. My. Word." Jules had gone into shock. She put her cup down altogether. "I'm not really on the phone, am I? This is some sort of dream?"

"Very funny," I replied.

"So what changed your mind? Who have you invited?" She held up crossed fingers. "Please say Oliver."

"The little boy I told you about. And his mum, Lizzie.

Although to be honest, it was more a case of Seb telling me they were coming."

Jules looked back at me, wearing the biggest of smiles. "It's a start, I suppose."

"So, do I get that menu or not?"

"Damn right, you do," Jules said. She paused and put a clenched hand to her mouth as if needing a moment. "Oh, Antonia, thank you. This is the best Christmas present ever."

"I'm not sure I'd go that far," I said.

"Year after year I worry about you being stuck indoors on your own, wishing you'd come to us. That for once, you'd celebrate with people around you. I know spending the holidays alone has always been your choice, but it's not healthy. Not really. And now I'm wittering." She reached down the side of her chair again and produced a tissue. "Honestly. I'm so pleased for you, Antonia, I could cry."

Watching her wipe her eyes, I suddenly felt guilty. I'd had no idea my keeping myself to myself over Christmas had caused Jules such concern. "Jules, I'm so sorry," I said, thinking about all the times I'd turned down her invitations. "If I'd known that's how you felt..."

Jules blew her nose into her tissue. "You can apologise later," she said. "Time's running out and we have work to do."

CHAPTER 33

Showered and dressed ready for a productive day, I made my way downstairs to the kitchen. I put the kettle on, before letting Frank out into the garden. Standing in the doorway watching him, I breathed in the cold countryside air. As I filled my lungs, I was surprised at how energised I felt. Especially when I couldn't say I'd had the best night's sleep.

Unable to stop thinking about Jules's response to the fact that I wouldn't be spending Christmas Day on my own that year, I'd lain awake for what seemed like hours. I could still see the tears in her eyes and the mix of relief and joy on her face when I'd told her about Seb and Lizzie coming round to celebrate. If I'd known Jules had hated me being on my own during the holidays to that extent, I'd have accepted every festive invitation she and Harry had given me. I felt so guilty, which probably explained why I let her run away with herself on the planning front. Then again, as I pictured her face as her ideas got bigger and bolder, I couldn't deny that I, too, had got carried away on her wave of enthusiasm.

Leaving Frank to his mooching, I poured the dog's breakfast

into his bowl. As I finished making my cup of coffee, I was determined to make up for the worry I'd caused. I might not be spending Christmas Day with my closest friends, but I was intent on doing them proud. I was going all out to make that year a Christmas to remember. My stomach lurched. Even if I had begun to regret agreeing to all of Jules's suggestions.

"Come on, Frank," I said. Calling him in, I thought of the numerous tasks on my Yuletide to-do list. "We have a very busy day ahead of us." I stood there, impatient, while he plodded inside, as if he didn't have a care in the world.

Closing the door behind Frank, I sifted through the pile of notes Jules had helped me put together. Menu, cooking instructions, order of works... I thanked goodness for my friend's ability to organise. I knew without such assistance, *I'd* have been stuffed, never mind the turkey. I looked at my list again. Goodness knew where I was going to get a Santa suit at that late stage.

Because it was my first time catering for Christmas, Jules hadn't only insisted I keep the menu simple, she'd made sure I could get ahead by doing most of the preparation on Christmas Eve. At the time, she'd made everything sound so easy, but looking at what I'd written, in the cold light of day it appeared anything but. My nerves began to creep in and having spent much of the previous night telling myself Christmas lunch would be a success, a little voice reminded me that doing the shopping, the cooking and playing host was the easy bit.

My phone bleeped and seeing the incoming text was from Oliver I couldn't help but smile as I picked it up. I took a deep breath, staring at the screen for a moment before opening his message.

Hope you enjoy today as much as I did yesterday. Maybe next time I can cook for you? xxx

Seeing the xxx on the end, I allowed myself a moment to consider our afternoon together. I sighed a dreamy sigh as I reread his words. Good looking, great kisser, and a dab hand in the kitchen. Was there anything that man couldn't do? I pulled myself together. "That's enough of that," I said. It was not the time to be daydreaming. "Come on, Frank. We've got places to go and people to see."

"I won't be a minute," I said to Frank, as he howled and yelped from Violet's front passenger seat. I didn't blame him for being excited to see me. I'd been in Wildeholt's supermarket for way longer than I'd anticipated. The poor dog must have thought he'd been deserted.

Struggling to control my trolley, I hoisted bag after bag into the back of the van. Having ticked off each item on my shopping list, I'd bought everything I needed for Christmas lunch and more. I smiled a satisfied smile as I lifted in the last of the carriers. Even if I turned out to be the worst host on the planet, it felt good to know my guests wouldn't starve.

With Christmas Day being so close and the store packed, I'd fully anticipated having to fight my way up and down the aisles, and squeeze through my fellow customers as I reached for the shelves. However, as I shut the van doors, got rid of my trolley, and climbed into the driving seat, I couldn't believe how well my shopping trip had gone. Patrons and staff alike had been polite; there'd been no angst in the air or catfighting over the last box of mince pies. And the choices to be made... Having never paid much attention before, I couldn't believe how many different kinds of Christmas pudding, tins of chocolates, and varieties of cake were available.

Naturally, I'd expected at least a couple of ingredients to

have sold out, leaving me no option but to traipse around shop after shop in search of an elusive bag of parsnips or sought-after carton of brandy sauce. But thanks to the supermarket staff, who'd done a sterling job on the shelf stacking front, my single concern was the size of the turkey I'd had to purchase. The only birds left were huge, leaving me no choice but to pick up a ten-pounder. I shook my head, all the while hoping my guests had healthy appetites. If not, I'd be force-feeding myself the damn thing from Christmas through to Easter.

I fired up Violet's engine, before putting her into gear and pulling out of the car park. Leaving Wildeholt behind, I began winding my way back to Little Leatherington. I turned on the radio to hear Mariah Carey's "All I want For Christmas" coming through the speakers, and as the DJ introduced Christmas hit after Christmas hit, I found myself joining in. I glanced around at my surroundings and as I ambled along one country road after another, for the first time since landing north, driving felt fun.

I fell silent when flashing lights in my rear-view mirror suddenly caught my attention and narrowing my eyes, I scowled at the driver behind. Beeping long and hard on his horn, the man was clearly trying to bully me into speeding up, but no matter his impatience, I refused to feel intimidated. Instead, I decided to let him pass and steered Violet over to the side accordingly so he could overtake. Going off his subsequent hand gestures, however, it was too little, too late. The man clearly thought I should have done that miles back. Shaking my head as I watched him disappear into the distance, I told myself there was no pleasing some people. However, after a quick glance at my speedometer, I fast found myself appreciating the man's frustration. I'd been driving thirty miles per hour on a sixty road, and I could have put my foot down a bit more if I'd wanted to.

I sighed, realising that, albeit on a subconscious level, I'd chosen to drive slower than necessary. Not only that, I knew the reason why. My heart sank as I considered my to-do list. I cursed Jules's eagerness, but also my stupidity for going along with it. It was all right for Jules; she enjoyed being the centre of attention; and she wasn't the one who risked being laughed out of town.

"Go big or go home," she'd said.

In that moment, I knew which I preferred.

Despite wishing I hadn't listened, I eased my foot down on the accelerator, insisting there was no point in delaying the inevitable. The sooner I got home, the sooner I got the worst of things out of the way.

It wasn't long before I landed back in Little Leatherington and pulling up outside Number 3, Bluebell Row, I steeled myself to lug all my shopping inside.

Getting out of the van, I opened up the cottage to let Frank inside, before returning to Violet. I opened her rear doors and stared at all the bags of food. "Here goes," I said. Reaching out, I pulled one towards me and grabbing a second, I carted them into the house. The bags dragged on my arms they were so heavy and by the time I got to the kitchen, the handles had dug into my hands. As I was returning for the next lot, a familiar Land Rover pulled up opposite, causing my heart to race.

Jason wound his window down to speak. "Need a hand?" he said.

I swallowed hard, before nodding. "Yes, please," I said, my voice cracking.

Jason nudged his brother who sat looking as miserable as ever in the driver's seat.

My pulse quickened further when, despite his apparent reluctance, Barrowboy unclipped his seat belt and just like Jason, got out to assist. I pictured Jules, willing me to get on with it and I took a deep breath. "It's now or never," I said, plastering a smile on my face.

CHAPTER 34

*C*arrying bag after bag, the three of us to-and-froed in and out of Number 3. Waiting for the opportunity to tick off another item on my to-do list, I felt nervous. I wasn't worried about Jason; he'd love my proposition. His brother was the issue. However, as Violet's rear became increasingly empty, I knew I had to say something and soon; before I missed the chance altogether.

"I love these," Jason said. Reaching into the van for his next haul, he indicated a box of Christmas crackers that poked out of one of the carriers. "Did you know they were invented back in 1846?"

I'd got used to Jason blurting out weird and wonderful Christmas facts, to the point that I looked forward to his festive titbits. Unlike Barrowboy, I noted, who having clearly heard all his brother's stories before, rolled his eyes, as he also reached for another bag.

"A chap called Tom Smith came up with the idea," Jason said. "At first, he wrapped up sweets, twisting the ends like you sometimes see even now. Then he added love messages into the wrapper.

"A love note, eh?" Barrowboy said. He looked my way. "Play your cards right, and you could be in line for one of those this year."

I stared at the man. He was obviously referring to my date with Oliver. However, that was the second time he'd intimated I was the source of local gossip and I smiled, refusing to let that latest remark pass. "I'm honoured," I said. "And there I was thinking you were saving yourself for Lizzie."

The man's face relaxed into a smile and as he got back to ferrying the shopping, I turned to Jason so he could finish his story.

"Anyway, when Tom Smith added the banger," Jason carried on. "He had to make an even bigger wrapper and after that, he swapped the sweets for a trinket."

"So it was a gradual process?" I asked.

"Very much so. It was his son, Walter Smith, who added the paper hats and jokes like we have today."

"Thank you for telling me," I said.

Jason grabbed the last of the bags and took them into the house, crossing paths with his brother in the hallway.

"That seems to be everything," Barrowboy said.

"Thank you," I replied. "I'd have had arms down to the floor if I'd had to shift it all myself."

Another flicker of a smile crossed the man's lips, but it was gone as quickly as it had arrived.

Jason reappeared and as Barrowboy nodded to the Land Rover, both men began to leave.

"Before you go…" I said. Seizing the moment, I pictured Jules cheering me on as I took a step towards them.

The two men stopped and turned to look my way.

"I wanted to ask you something?" Without yet knowing my question Barrowboy seemed uninterested, and my pulse quickened as a result. I plastered a smile on my face, ready to feel the fear and ask it anyway. "I was wondering if you'd both like to come for Christmas lunch?" I said.

Barrowboy looked at me like I'd gone mad.

I appreciated why, of course. I hardly knew the man and yet there I was, inviting him to spend the biggest day of the year with me.

In contrast, Jason's eyes lit up and his jaw dropped. He looked to his brother in anticipation, obviously desperate for the man to say yes.

"I don't think so," Barrowboy said.

Suddenly crestfallen, Jason let out a mournful sigh.

I recalled what Jason had said about not celebrating Christmas since his parents had passed away and my heart went out to him. It was evident Jason loved Christmastime, even if his brother didn't. Why else would he have committed all those unnecessary facts to memory? And despite missing out himself, Jason in no way begrudged anyone else celebrating. My eyes went from him to the tree in Aunt Lillian's window. If anything, he positively encouraged it.

I felt my hackles rise as without even an explanation, Barrowboy gestured to Jason once more, telling him to get in their vehicle. I'd known all along my question would be met less than positively, hence my reluctance to ask, but I couldn't help but wonder why the man had to be so rude? And, not that I dared say it, cruel? Deciding I had nothing to lose, I took another step forward. "Can I ask why?" I asked.

Again, Barrowboy stopped to look at me.

"Because while you might not enjoy Christmas, your brother here clearly does."

"It's all right, Antonia," Jason said.

"No, it's not. Because despite what anyone else might think, you count too, Jason." I returned my attention to Barrowboy. "As for you, I know you're busy with your farm and your mountain rescue stuff and whatever else it is you have going on, but have you ever thought that you might actually need a day off? That it would be good for you?" I indicated his brother. "That it would be good for both of you?" By then, not only did I have Barrowboy's attention, I was on a roll. "And it isn't as if this is *just* about either of you anyway. It's about a little boy who's scared witless because Christmas won't be the same this year." I pictured Seb's distress as he pleaded with Lizzie over coming to spend the day with me. "A little boy *and* his mother who have lived in this village for nearly a year now." I waved my arm around gesturing into the distance, as I recalled Lizzie's panic at the bus stop. "Who still don't know anyone. Talk about community spirit." I folded my arms and closed my eyes for a moment to settle myself. "I just thought," I said, my voice calmer. "It would be nice if they got to know some of their neighbours. I'll be gone soon and what with you two being a couple of the few locals I've met…"

Barrowboy stared at me, silent.

"Please, Barrowboy," Jason said. "I can help with the milking first thing. Help with whatever else needs sorting. And if you can't do it for me, then do it for Seb and Lizzie." He stared at his brother, his eyes pleading.

Barrowboy looked both shocked and hurt. "Why wouldn't I do it for you?" he said, his voice pained. "You're my brother. You matter more than anyone."

"You say that, but…"

Barrowboy stepped forward and pulled his brother into a bear hug. "Don't you ever think otherwise." He held on tight.

"Although I'm not being completely selfless," I said, picturing the ten-pounds-worth of turkey sandwiches I might have to eat. "You've seen for yourself the size of that bird in there."

Barrowboy finally let go of his brother. "What time do you want us?" he asked.

CHAPTER 35

*A*s I put away my shopping, I felt relieved to have got Jason and Barrowboy's invitation out of the way. I'd known Jason would jump at the chance to celebrate Christmas no matter the circumstances; his brother had been the one to cause me trepidation. I'd seen hints at a softer side to Barrowboy, but on the whole he seemed such a serious, almost gruff, individual. As guests went, I just hoped he wasn't going to be too difficult, particularly when I was nervous about cooking for a bunch of people I hardly knew to begin with.

While Jules had assured me the menu was simple, taking in the many ingredients and elements involved I could see how easy it would be for Christmas lunch to go wrong. But I told myself to focus on the positives and that, despite my lack of confidence, no matter how things turned out I was doing a good thing. Thanks to Jules's Yuletide enthusiasm and my stupidity for going along with it, not only did Lizzie and Seb have the chance to build relationships in the village, Jason would be celebrating Christmas for the first time in I didn't know how long.

A picture of Ted popped into my head. Like Barrowboy, he wasn't always the most amenable of people either. I sighed. When it came to the old man and his role in my plan, I supposed I'd just have to wait and see.

Pushing all potential problems to the back of my mind, I decided to focus on logistics. My immediate question being, where everyone was going to sit. The kitchen table wasn't big enough for us all to squeeze around and even if it were, the room itself was too cramped. I hadn't thought about seating arrangements when I'd agreed to Seb and Lizzie coming for lunch, let alone when I'd made the decision to invite the others. I looked out into the garden and not yet ready to ask everyone to bring their own chair, I prayed for divine intervention.

"I wonder..." I said, as my eyes settled on the stone outbuilding at the far end.

Going off everyone's descriptions, Jules's Aunt Lillian had been an outgoing person, so had to have entertained at some point. Aware that she was also a bit of a hoarder, it stood to reason that she might have stored all her extra bits and pieces out there. Extras that might have included dining chairs.

I told myself there was no time like the present and exiting the house to go and check, I folded my arms over my chest as I walked. It was freezing out there and icy underfoot and as I tiptoed along trying not to slip, I hoped the trek was worth it. I approached the outbuilding door and trying the handle, was pleased to find it unlocked. Entering, I filled my cheeks with air and exhaled. Just like Aunt Lillian's house, the space was a pure treasure trove. Scanning the room, I couldn't believe how huge it was. Even crammed with stuff, the building looked bigger on the inside than it did out; it was a veritable Tardis. Had it been in London, it would have been perfect for my roadside reclamation business.

I glimpsed a couple of chairs towards the back and moving a few dusty old boxes out of the way, I managed to clear a path so I could get to them. Placing them side by side, I sat on one and then the other, shuffling my bum about on each to check their sturdiness. Satisfied they were solid, I stood up again and dusted myself down before giving them a closer inspection. While both appeared to be made of oak, one was a ladder-back design and the other lath, so they definitely weren't a pair. I smiled. After getting rid of the cobwebs and giving them a good wash down, they'd be perfect for Christmas Day.

As I moved a few more boxes, to try and find other suitable seating and, fingers crossed, a table, my eyes widened at the sight of an original Singer sewing machine complete with ornate metal foot trestle. I ran a finger through the thick coating of dust that had accumulated on its wooden top, before taking a peek inside the cavity beneath. I grinned, glad to see the appliance still intact. Looking around, I took in a fabulous old pot sink, upon which balanced a red fibreglass kayak and next to that an old gas camping stove. I giggled and thinking of Lillian's adventurous spirit I readily imagined her pegging a tent, ready to enjoy a weekend's canoeing on the open water. An old-fashioned tin bath lay tucked in one corner and again I thought of Jules's aunt. As a child, it could well have been something she'd used.

I shivered, feeling the cold once more, and telling myself I'd come back to the workshop another day for a proper scout around, I picked up the two chairs and carried them outside. Making sure to close the door tight behind me, I headed along the path to the house.

Back in the kitchen, I rummaged under the sink for a cloth and filling the sink with hot soapy water, I gave the chairs a thorough wash. Drying them off with a tea towel, I began to see the beauty of the wood coming through. But while such warm shades of patina made my heart sing, I still didn't have enough seating. "Then again..." I said, after a moment's thought.

Remembering Ted Sharples's offer, I wondered if it was time to act like the roadside reclamation specialist I claimed to be. While Oliver had said the old man's skip probably wouldn't contain anything worth salvaging, I knew I should check it out just in case. Plus, popping up there would enable me to get the next step in my plan organised, I realised. At least I hoped it would. Reminding myself that Ted wasn't always the most amenable of characters, I chewed on my lip. It was a big ask.

In what felt like a now or never moment, I headed out into the hall and grabbed my coat off the bottom of the banister. "I won't be long, Frank," I said, nipping into the lounge.

Snoring away, the dog laid on his back, legs in the air, with his head to one side and his tongue hanging out.

I chuckled at the sight. It seemed Frank wasn't coming with me even if I wanted him to. Leaving him to his dreams, I made my way out to the van and climbed in.

Still warm from the trip to the supermarket, Violet's engine easily started up and driving out of the village, I began winding my way up into the hills. A layer of snow gradually began to appear on the road, forcing me to slow down and grip the steering wheel as I snaked up through the hamlet, pleased to see that there were no nosey neighbours to contend with. I left the collection of houses behind and ascended higher still, until I reached the stretch of never-ending road. Staring ahead, I knew the old farmhouse was situated along there somewhere. It was just a case of finding it.

"There you are," I said, at last, spotting Ted's bright yellow skip. It stood proud against the surrounding snow-covered grasslands and pulling up in front of it, I took a moment to gather myself. I looked up to the house to see Ted at the window and as he looked my way, I didn't even get a smile, never mind a wave acknowledging my presence. Realising there was no going back, my shoulders slumped. If the man was in a bad mood before I'd spoken to him, I dreaded to think how he'd feel afterwards.

CHAPTER 36

*T*ed was already at the door by the time I reached the farmhouse entrance and seeing him stood there stony-faced did nothing to alleviate my anxiety. I told myself not to be so soft. I'd handled his attitude before and just because we were on his turf, that didn't mean I couldn't handle it again.

"Antonia," he said.

"What? Don't I even get a smile?"

The responding twinkle in his eye told me he was teasing and that under the façade, he was, in fact, happy to see me. I shook my head at his behaviour, as he chuckled and stepped aside to let me in, at the same time gesturing our way down the hall.

Entering the house, I passed by two closed doors, one to my left and one to my right. Pictures lined the hallway walls, but what really caught my attention were the beautiful Victorian floor tiles. Made up of a small black and cream chequered pattern, they were edged in a contrasting triangular design.

Continuing into the kitchen, I couldn't believe how spacious it was. Taking in the huge farmhouse table in the centre, I wouldn't have been surprised if my whole London flat fit in that one room alone. I immediately felt the warmth that was, no doubt, emanating from the Aga in the chimney breast opposite. There was a butler sink with brass tap fittings under the window to my right and a huge Welsh dresser sat to my left displaying all kinds of crockery, from a gravy boat to a stack of teacups. Ted's kitchen units were made of stripped pine, as was the huge built-in plate rack. With a pile of washing up in the sink, a discarded half-eaten sandwich, and what was clearly an original terracotta floor in need of a mop, it wasn't the tidiest of spaces. But it was a proper working kitchen, not a showroom. I had a real sense of being in the heart of Ted's home.

Ted followed me in, just as the well-used kettle on the stove began to shrill. The sound pierced my eardrums so it was a relief when he picked it up off the heat and carried it over to a worktop trivet.

"Just in time," he said. "Will tea do you?"

"That would be lovely," I replied. As I hovered near the doorway, he dropped a couple of teabags into a huge brown teapot and filled it with the freshly boiled water.

"Come to root in that skip, have you?" he asked, as he concentrated on the task at hand.

"If that's all right with you, yes." Knowing full well that wasn't the sole reason for my visit, I took in the man's solemnity. Ted had proven himself to be less than sociable on more than one occasion and what I wanted from him called for anything but. I decided to wait for the right moment before asking. The last thing I wanted was for him to laugh me out of the door.

He positioned two mugs on a tray, along with the teapot and a sugar bowl. "Don't just stand there," he said. "Sit yourself down." He placed the tray on the table, and while I did as I was told and took a seat, he went to fetch a biscuit barrel from the kitchen counter. "Help yourself," he said. Joining me, he sat down too and took a sip of his drink. "Looking for anything in particular?" he asked.

"Dining chairs and a table," I said.

"Ha! Isn't everyone at this time of year?"

I smiled. The man had a point.

Ted suddenly appeared wistful. "When I think of the Christmases we've had around this beauty." He ran his hand over the well-worn wooden surface in front of him. "The wife loved this time of year. Not that we did anything fancy. It was only ever the three of us. Her, me and Ollie..."

I smiled at the shortening of his grandson's name, at the same time wondering where Oliver's parents would be if not there.

"We raised him," Ted said, as if reading my mind. "His mum, Sam, our daughter, passed away when he was a baby."

Both saddened and surprised to hear that, my heart skipped a beat. "I'm so sorry," I replied. "That's awful." For me, the pain of losing a parent had been gut-wrenching enough. For Ted and his wife, losing a child must have been unbearable. And poor Oliver, to have never known his own mother.

I thought back to my first meeting with Oliver, when he'd asked me if I was Italian, leaving me no choice but to explain that mum was an Antonio Banderas superfan. I recalled his expression when I went on to say she'd since died. The understanding he showed obviously came from experience. Although compared to him, I was lucky. I got to know my mum.

"As for Ollie's dad," Ted carried on. "Well, he's never been on the scene. He scarpered quicker than it took for the blue line to appear on the pregnancy test. I think that was one of the reasons the wife insisted we went all out. Only at birthdays and Christmas, mind. We didn't spoil the lad."

I smiled, betting they did.

"You know, to make up for the fact that Ollie was stuck with us old cronies." Despite his joking, there was a real tenderness in Ted's voice. "At Christmastime, you'd have thought the wife was feeding the five thousand. When it came to food, that woman was a miracle worker. She really could make something out of nothing." He took another mouthful of tea, as if needing a moment to pull himself together. "It's not the same now, of course. Although me and Ollie do our best." He laughed as if recalling more recent Christmases past. "We muddle through." Ted lowered his gaze and running a finger along the rim of his cup, looked at me through his eyelashes. "Maybe when that grandson of mine has his own family we'll get back to having fun again," he said, his tone pointed.

I immediately knew what the man was getting at and as I put my cup to my lips, my tea went down the wrong hole. Forced to cough my way out of it, Ted continued to play innocent.

"I miss those days. I wouldn't get away with pretending to be Santa now. Not at the age Ollie's at."

"You played Santa?"

Ted smiled. "When he was small, yes." His smile turned to a chuckle. "I'm not saying he wasn't a bright lad, but not once did he click it was me."

Watching Ted laugh, my senses heightened. Yes, the old man had thick white hair and a fuzzy beard, but I was seeing a new side to him and it wasn't just Ted's appearance that made him the perfect Father Christmas.

"I've still got the red suit somewhere."

"Really?" I asked. Sitting there, I tried to look casual. "Does it still fit?"

Ted's eyes narrowed and he looked at me direct. "Probably. Why do you ask?" I shifted in my seat, while he put a hand up to stroke his beard. "You didn't just come here for a table and some chairs, did you?"

I screwed up my face. "To be honest," I said. "No."

CHAPTER 37

"Come on then," Ted said. "Spit it out."

Realising his response to my request could go either way, I steeled myself ready to explain. "There's this woman in the village. She's on her own with her son, Seb. He's seven years old and this is their first Christmas just the two of them. His dad's no longer around. Let's just say he's moved on."

"Ah," Ted said, his eyebrows raised. "Another one of those, eh?"

"Well, Seb's already questioning Santa Claus's existence, so there's a good chance that next year he won't believe in him at all..." I took a sip of my tea.

"So you want this year to be a year to remember?"

"I do. Plus, I'm hoping to take his mind off the fact that his dad won't be around."

"I see," Ted said.

"His mum doesn't know anything about this, by the way, so it's okay if you say no. I just thought maybe you could help?"

"By playing the role of Father Christmas?" Ted said.

"Yes. On Christmas Eve. Like you did way back when. For Oliver." Hoping the mention of his grandson would swing it, I wrinkled my nose in anticipation. "Seb's such a lovely little boy and with only a couple of days to go, I know it's short notice. And I understand if you'd rather not and like I said, I haven't mentioned any of this to Lizzie. So no one will be any the wiser, if you..."

"Okay," Ted said, his face serious. "I'll do it."

"You will?" I took in the man's continued sternness. "And you'll *Ho! Ho! Ho*?" I asked, needing to make sure. "Because nobody likes a grumpy Santa."

"If I have to." Ted held his stern expression for a second or two longer, before his face broke into a smile. "Of course, I'll *Ho! Ho! Ho!*" he said. "I wouldn't be doing my job if I didn't."

Relief swept over me and I jumped up from my seat, raced around the table and threw my arms around Ted. "Thank you," I said. "You don't know how much this means to me."

"How much what means?" asked Oliver. Suddenly appearing in the doorway, he took in the sight of me hugging his granddad. "What's going on?"

"Two visitors in one day. I am lucky," Ted said.

I straightened up, my face beaming. It was the first time I'd seen Oliver since our trip to Missingham House. Since our kiss. Just the thought of it and I had to will myself not to blush. "Your granddad's just said he'll play Father Christmas."

"Really?" He looked from Ted to me, his surprise obvious. "For who?"

"A little boy I know."

Looking impressed, Oliver took off his coat. Placing it over a chair, he walked straight towards me and leaning in, kissed my cheek.

My tummy flipped as his lips brushed my skin. After which, with all the resolve in the world, I couldn't stop my cheeks from flushing.

"How did you get him to agree to that?" he said, winking at me.

I flushed even more.

Oliver looked at the old man. "Are you feeling okay? You're not sick, are you?"

"Cheeky," Ted said.

Watching the two of them, I couldn't help but think their interaction sweet. And while Oliver was the same gorgeous man he'd been when I first met him, Ted bore no resemblance to the grouchy individual I'd met on my first visit to The Cobblestone Tavern. "Look, I'm glad you're both here." I took a deep breath. "I didn't just call in because of the skip and to ask you, Ted, for a favour."

"You mean there's more?" Ted said.

As the two of them waited for me to continue, my mouth suddenly felt dry and I wondered what was wrong with me. Tempted to chicken out for fear of rejection, I reminded myself that Jules would never let me hear the end of it if I did. "I wondered if you both fancied Christmas dinner at Number 3 this year," I said.

Oliver's face broke into a smile. Ted appeared surprised.

"I mean it won't be as good as Mrs Sharples's, but going off the size of the turkey I might just be able to feed the five thousand."

"You know about Grandma's festive miracles? You two have been talking," Oliver looked from me to his grandfather. "I hope you haven't been speaking out of turn," he said.

"Never," Ted replied, smiling my way. I stayed quiet about his great-grandchild comment.

"So what do you think, Granddad? Shall we risk it?"

Ted shrugged. "It's either that or we're muddling through again."

"Don't speak too soon, Ted. This is my first time entertaining."

Oliver looked at me, his expression warm. "We'd love to."

Relief swept over me. I wouldn't have been able to bear the embarrassment if they'd declined my invitation. "Good. Barrowboy and Jason are joining us too."

"They are?" Oliver asked, surprised.

I recalled my outburst when I'd more or less called Barrowboy selfish. "To be fair, I did railroad your friend into it."

Oliver laughed.

"Then there's Lizzie and Seb. Seb's the little boy Ted's playing dress-up for."

"Isn't she the lady Barrowboy just happens to be interested in?"

"Yes, well, that's sort of a bonus," I said, laughing.

I turned to Ted. Ready to swing into action, I put on my roadside reclamation specialist hat, knowing that without chairs and a table, we'd all be balancing lunch on our knees. "About that skip," I said.

CHAPTER 38

*I*t was the day after my visit to Ted's farmhouse. I wasn't long back from a frantic last-minute shopping trip and Ted had just telephoned. My heart skipped a beat when I'd heard his voice and, worried he'd rung to tell me he'd changed his mind about playing Santa, a moment of panic had set in. My relief was palpable when he proudly declared that, yes, his Santa suit did still fit, and that it was all systems go for the following evening. I'd got straight on the phone to Lizzie to give her the rundown on our plans for both Seb and Christmas Day.

"I can't believe you're doing all this for us." The surprise in Lizzie's voice was undeniable. "It's so kind of you."

Thankfully Seb was spending the day with his dad so Lizzie and I were able to talk freely.

"And you're definitely sure you don't mind?" I asked. "Because if I've overstepped the mark, you can tell me. I won't be offended."

I considered my own Christmases past, recalling the times when people went above and beyond for me and mum. Neighbours often claimed to have a couple of spare pantomime

189

tickets we might've wanted, or to have inadvertently found themselves with more presents to give out than needed. Of course, mum knew such gifts weren't really mere oversights and although gracious in her response, she hated the fact that we were viewed as a charity case. Not that I thought Lizzie and Seb were penniless. I just wanted Seb's first Christmas without his father to be a more positive experience than the little boy anticipated.

Lizzie let out a laugh. "Why would I mind? I think what you've organised is wonderful."

Admittedly, I had been worrying about what Lizzie might think. I'd questioned if I should have spoken to her about my intentions, instead of getting everything organised first. "I just wanted to make sure Ted was up for the role before mentioning it," I said. "I'd have felt awful if I'd opened my mouth, you'd got excited and then he turned around and said no."

"If anything, I'm grateful, Antonia. Thank you," Lizzie said. "For everything. I know Seb didn't give you much of a choice about having us over, which I feel awful about, by the way. I just wish he'd told me what was going on in that little head of his."

"He probably didn't want to upset you."

"He's all right now. We had a bit of a chat and he can't wait for Christmas Day. As for him having his own special visit from Santa. That really will be the icing on the cake." She giggled. "I can't wait to see his face. It's certainly going to be a Christmas to remember."

The joy in Lizzie's voice was heart-warming. "I wish I could take all the credit," I replied. "Inviting everyone else was Jules's suggestion. She's a friend from back home. I've known her since forever. Once I told her you and Seb were coming for Christmas lunch, things sort of snowballed. It's a Christmas swap kind of thing. Instead of going full on this year, she's having a quiet day.

And vice versa when it comes to me. Jules is also the one who came up with the idea for Santa's visit."

"She sounds fun," Lizzie said.

I pictured my friend's enthusiasm, not just for all things Yuletide, but for life itself. "She is. If you ever fancy a trip to London, I'll introduce you."

"It's a deal."

I laughed. "I've just realised how bossy I've made her sound. And I'm not really just doing as I'm told. Honestly."

Lizzie chuckled, before letting out a long sigh. "I'm going to miss you when you leave," she said.

I smiled. Although as kind as that was of her to say, I doubted it. Recalling her first introduction to Barrowboy, Christmas Day was going to be interesting. And if things worked out in the way I hoped, she would be too busy getting to know him to miss me. "You haven't tasted my cooking yet," I said. "You won't be saying that when you're in the hospital with food poisoning."

Lizzie laughed again. "You're sure you can't hang around a bit longer? I know Seb and I aren't the only ones who'd like that. From what I hear, our local letting agent will be pretty gutted if you go."

I smiled. Knowing where that snippet of information had to have come from; it was good to know Lizzie and Barrowboy were still chatting and getting to know each other. "You shouldn't believe everything you're told," I said.

I could almost hear Lizzie's eye-roll.

"Right, I suppose I should go," I said. "I've got some chairs to clean up."

"Is there anything I can do to help? Anything you need?"

I glanced at the pile of notes on the coffee table. Taking in the numerous ticks scribbled all over them, I seemed to have everything covered. I pictured myself earlier that day, hotfooting it around Wildeholt, going from shop to shop to shop, picking up all the little extras I'd wanted. My only disappointment was having to buy a wallpaper pasting table for everyone to sit at. Still, at least thanks to Ted and his skip everyone had a proper chair. "I don't think so," I replied. My eyes were drawn to the pile of presents, wrapped and labelled under the Christmas tree. I smiled at the sight. My bank account might have taken a battering, but I'd had lots of fun in the process. Finally, I appreciated the last-minute buzz that Jules had talked about when it came to her Christmas preparations. "I appear to be on track."

After ending our call, I turned my attention to the space around me, wondering where I was going to put the table and chairs. Aunt Lillian's cottage didn't have its own dining room and the kitchen was way too small to cater for seven. That only left the lounge in which to seat everyone. I picked up one end of the coffee table and dragged it into position against the wall next to the sideboard and while maintaining the same configuration for the three-piece suite, I simply moved the sofa and armchairs nearer to the fire. "Very cosy," I said. Standing back to assess the overall effect, I shook my head at Frank who lay cocooned in the centre of them.

The dog continued to laze in front of the flames, not even opening his eyes at the sound of my voice. Looking at him, I frowned, unable to believe how immobile Frank had become. I knew Jules was going to wonder what I'd done to him when we got back to London, because gone was the energetic little hound she'd entrusted in my care. In a matter of weeks, he turned into the canine equivalent of a couch potato.

CHAPTER 39

Christmas Eve

*W*ith a busy Christmas Eve ahead, I got up early and took Frank out before I'd even had my first cup of coffee. The sky looked ominous and thanks to a freezing wind, the air felt bitter. As usual, Frank didn't seem to notice the sub-zero temperature and while I tried to chivvy him along, he dug his feet in at every opportunity, more than happy to stay out in the cold. I, on the other hand, couldn't wait to get back indoors and refused to give in to his delay tactics. Tug after tug on his lead, I finally got him to Number 3.

As soon as we were inside, I went straight to work on the fire. Rolling up my sleeves, I cleaned and lit it, before heading into the kitchen to make a hot drink. Glancing at the pile of notes on the counter awaiting my attention, I told myself to warm up first. With lots to do, I'd be busy soon enough. After carrying my coffee into the lounge, I plonked myself on the sofa and sipped on my drink, while the heat from the flames worked its magic.

Sitting there in the quiet, I thought about my Christmas Day guests. We were such a varied bunch that I couldn't imagine how we'd all relate. Thanks to our differences, conversation around the dinner table would either be interesting, stilted, or worst-case scenario, non-existent. I smiled, thankful that Jason and Seb would be present. Recalling our tree decorating afternoon, I doubted either of those two would sit in silence for long.

I didn't know how Jules did it year after year. Having a quiet day would certainly be a new experience for her; I only hoped it was a positive one. Fingers crossed, mine would be too. Hosting Christmas lunch felt like a big responsibility and the more I thought about it, the more my nerves began to creep in. I refused to let them take hold. Considering the ups and downs I'd already gone through since landing in Little Leatherington, nothing could be worse than getting stuck up a mountain or mistaking a cow for a burglar. I sighed dreamily, reflecting on one of the more positive aspects of my stay. Or beat being kissed by Mr Oliver Chase.

Shaking myself out of it, I picked up my phone and searched YouTube for the ultimate Christmas number one playlist. Whacking up the volume to full, I rose to my feet and ready to dance and sing my way through a whole host of jobs, headed out to the kitchen.

My singing paused as, holding it at arm's length, I heaved the huge turkey onto the trivet of onion, carrots, celery, and garlic that lay in the bottom of a roasting tray. Looking at it sat there, all pink and raw, I grimaced, unable to believe how much manhandling I'd done. Forced to rid the bird of its giblets, before stuffing and buttering the thing, I realised I'd never make a butcher. I pulled off my greasy surgical gloves and tossed them into the bin, continuing to scowl as I covered the turkey in tinfoil ready to go in the bottom of the fridge.

I turned on the sink's hot tap and soaped my hands up under the steaming water to get rid of any potential food poisoning bugs, at the same time considering how my to-do list fared. My smile returned. I'd had a busy morning and having already parboiled and fluffed up the potatoes, washed peeled and chopped the vegetables, and made a creamy, booze-laden trifle following Jules's special recipe, I seemed to be on target with my preparations. My mouth watered. I could have eaten that dessert there and then.

Telling myself I'd have to make do with a cup of coffee and a well-deserved biscuit, I flicked on the kettle and delved in the cupboard. I frowned as I took in all the goodies before me. A Christmas pudding, a Christmas cake, after-dinner mints... There was everything for the big day itself, but as I pushed aside a box of mince pies for a better look, there wasn't a simple biscuit in sight. Tempted to choose something from what was there, my hand hovered over a bag of chocolate coins that I had bought for Seb. However, I couldn't steal from a child and it would only take minutes to nip to the shop. So I whipped my hand away before I could change my mind.

I made my way out into the hall, put on my coat, and popped my head into the lounge to see Frank fast asleep in front of the fire. I chuckled at the sound of his snoring and deciding to leave him be, headed for the front door. The air temperature seemed to have further plummeted and as I set off down the street, I began to wish I'd opened Seb's chocolate coins after all. I stuffed my hands deep inside my pockets as I walked and picking up pace, told myself the quicker I got to the shop, the quicker I would be back.

As I neared my destination, I wasn't surprised to see Flat Cap Man loitering opposite.

Stood there in the freezing cold with a bunch of flowers, he was giving himself his usual pep talk as he paced first left and then right.

My heart went out to him and recalling what Oliver had said about the chap's feelings for the shopkeeper, Marianne, I wished Flat Cap Man would pluck up the courage to ask her out once and for all. Not only for his sake, but hers too, I reasoned. It couldn't be good for the woman to have her head stuck in a book all the time, instead of engaging with real people in the real world.

You're one to talk, a little voice reminded me.

I scoffed and for the first time since landing in Little Leatherington, I didn't just listen to my inner critic, I agreed.

Jules had been right to say I wasn't a people person. That was why I loved living in London. London gave me anonymity. I didn't stand out. I was a tiny little pixel in a massively big picture. I spent my days avoiding everyone around me. Apart from Harry and Jules, that was. I didn't even know my neighbours. No wonder Jules had finally forced me out of my comfort zone by sending me to a place like Little Leatherington, where I couldn't hide in a sea of people. Being a southerner in the north and a city woman in the countryside, I was always going to stand out. Whether I wanted to or not. Of course, the predicaments I'd found myself in had made me even more conspicuous.

Approaching the shop, I gave Flat Cap Man a wave. "Merry Christmas," I said to him, before entering.

Searching for a packet of biscuits, I made my choice and headed to the till where Marianne and her reindeer deely boppers enjoyed their latest read. I coughed to get her attention, but just like on every other occasion it was to no avail. I looked out of the window at Flat Cap Man, who continued to pace and give himself a good talking to. Returning my gaze to the shopkeeper, it was clear the situation called for direct action. I checked the price of my purchase and dug out the exact amount from my pocket and after placing it on the counter, I reached over and took Marianne's book from her hand.

"What the...?" she said. After two weeks of trying, I, at last, had the woman's attention.

"It's all there," I said, smiling as I nodded to my payment.

"Thank you," Marianne replied. Scooping up the coins, she rang up the till and dropped the money into its drawer, her expression a mix of annoyance and confusion throughout. "Is that everything?" she asked.

"Not quite, no," I said. I opened the shop door and remembering Oliver had mentioned Flat Cap Man's name, called out to him. "Lewis!"

He looked my way.

"Could you come here, please."

The poor man was mortified. He looked from me to down the street, as if tempted to do a runner.

"Now," I said, using my sternest of voices.

Realising he didn't have a choice in the matter, he tentatively stepped into the road and made his approach.

I took him by the arm and gently guided him inside the store. "Marianne, this is Lewis."

Lewis stood there dumbfounded, clearly in awe of the woman, while Marianne sat there wide-eyed, understandably wondering what was going on.

"He has something for you. Don't you, Lewis?"

He looked at me, as if not sure what to do.

I nodded to the flowers he carried.

"Oh, yes," he said. He stepped forward, holding them out for Marianne to take.

"For me?" she asked, surprised.

Lewis nodded and his cheeks reddened.

"Really?" Accepting them, Marianne's face broke into a smile.

Her shocked yet appreciative expression seemed to give Lewis's confidence the boost it needed. "They're gerbera daisies," he said. "I thought they were pretty, just like you."

Marianne appeared bashful. "Thank you," she said. "No one's ever bought me flowers before."

Feeling quite pleased with myself, I placed the shopkeeper's book down on the counter. "Merry Christmas," I said, as I stepped towards the door.

Too busy focusing on each other, neither seemed to hear me, but that didn't matter. Happy to leave them to it, I made my exit.

CHAPTER 40

"I can't believe you played matchmaker," Jules said. "When I think of all the complaints you make when I do the same for you. You hate anything like that."

I took in my friend's amused disbelief. Watching her get on with the last of her present wrapping, I was surprised to find the woman was still sane, let alone happy. After weeks and weeks spent in that chair, the Jules I knew and loved should have been downright miserable. "Someone had to step in," I said. "Because as desperate as the man was to get to know Marianne, left to his own devices it was never going to happen."

Jules stopped what she was doing to look at me direct. "Which is exactly what I say."

I let out a chuckle, knowing she was right.

"Marianne," she said, with a sigh. "You even know the woman's name." Jules put down her gift packaging altogether. She again looked straight at me. "I'm so proud of you, Antonia. A few weeks ago, no way would you have interfered like that. You'd have said it was none of your business. Maybe I was wrong and you're a people person, after all." She giggled. "Or maybe I was right, and you just needed to find your circle."

I shook my head and smiled. Despite the contradiction, Jules had accused me of both. Observing her as she talked, I wondered if I was imagining the glistening fluid that had developed in the corner of her eyes. Concerned she was about to cry, I questioned if I'd been mistaken when it came to the state of her well-being and that she wasn't happy at all.

"I honestly thought you'd lock yourself away, pretending to research your skip ratting business," Jules carried on.

"Roadside reclamation specialist."

"Same thing."

I decided to let it pass.

"But instead, you're out and about making friends. As for Christmas Day..."

"You're the one who suggested the Christmas swap," I said. "In fact, it's because of you mine's grown into what it is." I recalled her ever-increasing excitement as she kept adding to my invitation list, the way she clapped her hands together as she came up with the idea for Santa Claus's visit, and her detailed instructions as she outlined her suggested menu.

"But I didn't expect you to go for it. Then again, I suppose you were already halfway there thanks to little Sebbie."

I cocked my head, suddenly confident that, yes, the woman was losing it. "Little who?" I asked.

"Speaking of Christmas, how are things going? Are you organised?"

"As much as I can be. All the food prep is sorted. Once I've set the table, I think I've done everything I can for today." I flicked through my notes to make sure. "Then it's just a case of getting ready for tonight."

Jules's shoulders slumped. "I wish I could be there," she said. "Little Sebbie's face is going to be a picture."

I wished she'd stop calling him that.

"Oh, to believe in Father Christmas and all his magic at this time of year." She sighed. "Antonia, why do we have to grow up?"

I let out a nervous laugh. Jules's mood seemed to be all over the place.

Jules pulled herself together and quickly changed the subject. "So, are you looking forward to seeing the gorgeous Mr Chase later?" she asked.

"I am," I said, cautious. The way she was behaving, I almost dreaded the woman's response.

Jules's eyes narrowed. "What? No blushing, no dismissing, no head-shaking at the mere suggestion you might like the man?"

"Nope."

She looked at me, suspicious. "There's something in the water, isn't there? Either that, or there's been an alien abduction and I'm not looking at the real Antonia here. I've never seen you so... so..." She stopped speaking for a moment. "I think I'm going to cry."

While Jules reached for a tissue and dabbed her eyes, I remembered her tears during our last video call.

"I'm sorry," she said. "I can't seem to help it. I'm just so happy for you."

Feeling bad for my friend, my body crumpled at the sight of her sobbing, before it tensed again at the unnecessary noise as she blew her nose. "Jules, are you sure you're all right? I mean you have been confined to the house for a good while now. Maybe you should think about getting out into the fresh air?"

"I'm fine," Jules said. She grabbed another tissue and gave her eyes a final wipe. "Although I am feeling a bit fed up sat here all day."

I knew it. "Have you told Harry it's getting a bit much?"

"Oh, yes," she replied, deadly serious.

I couldn't help but smile. After her little outburst, I wasn't sure who to sympathise with more – Jules or her husband?

"He says it's my hormones."

"Hormones?" I looked at her confused. "What have they got to do with a broken leg?"

Jules wrinkled her nose as she looked at me.

"No," I said. As the penny began to drop, I covered my mouth with my hand, hiding my grin just in case I was wrong.

Jules's smile beamed. She nodded. "Yes. I'm pregnant."

I screamed and bounced up and down in my seat with joy, causing Frank to lift his head and let out a short sharp bark, before settling back down again. "Since when? Why am I only hearing about this now?"

"Oh you, know. That whole *keep things to yourself until a certain point just in case* thing. Although to be fair, we only found out a couple of weeks ago, so it hasn't been a secret for long."

"Even so," I said. I didn't know how she'd managed to keep quiet at all.

"You don't mind us not telling you, do you?" Jules asked.

"Of course, I don't."

"Because as well as wanting to make sure nothing, well, you know... I think we just wanted the baby to ourselves for a short while."

"Aw, that's so lovely." Tears welled in my own eyes, but with no hanky to hand, I'd no choice but to make use of my sweater sleeves. "I'm so pleased for you both. Harry must be delighted."

Jules smiled. "He is."

"I wish I could give you both a hug," I said, telling myself January would be round before I knew it.

"Look, I should let you go," Jules said. "You've got a table to lay, and a Santa visit to get ready for."

"Okay," I said. I smiled at my friend, unable to believe that she was starting her own family. "I'll speak to you tomorrow, yeah. To wish you both – or should I say all three of you, a happy Christmas."

As we ended our call, I couldn't stop grinning.

Frank let out a long, pitiful whine.

I chuckled. Having been the centre of attention himself since he was a puppy, no wonder he wasn't happy.

CHAPTER 41

*I*hadn't been able to stop smiling following my call with Jules. As I put the finishing touches to the dining table, news of her and Harry's pregnancy felt like the best Christmas present they could have given me. I knew they were going to make wonderful parents and I'd never felt so happy for them.

I stood back to admire my efforts. There was no sign of the wallpaper pasting table I'd had to buy during that morning's visit to Wildeholt. Thanks to Aunt Lillian's stash of beautiful coverings, it sat hidden under a brilliant white cotton cloth. And the mismatched crockery I'd laid out looked wonderful in its disparity. Made up of antique and near antique pieces in both bone china and ironstone ware, there were various designs. From Royal Albert to Mason, from RH & SL Plant to Royal Doulton, there hadn't been a complete dinner service amongst them. What was complete though, was the set of Waterford crystal wine glasses. As was the canteen of silverware. I took a deep breath and let out a contented sigh, more than pleased with how the ensemble had come together. "Perfectly imperfect," I said. "Just like my guests."

I checked my watch to see if I had time for a quick shower before heading round to Lizzie and Seb's, but both it and a knock at the door told me I didn't. I looked down at my sweater and jeans, before putting a hand up to straighten my untidy hair. Like it or not, I'd just have to do.

Heading out to answer the door, I opened it to find Oliver stood there. Wrapped up in a black woollen thigh-length coat and wearing a beanie, he looked gorgeous as ever. "You ready?" he asked.

Frank came racing out of the lounge at the sound of Oliver's voice.

"Someone's honoured," I said, as Oliver reached down and gave the dog a fuss. "I haven't been able to get him to move all day." I reached for Frank's lead and passed it to Oliver and while he secured it to the dog's collar, I grabbed my coat and put on my bobble hat and gloves.

"Very fetching," Oliver said, taking in my ensemble.

"And practical," I replied. "If I thought it was cold before, that's nothing to what it feels like tonight."

Closing the door behind us, we set off to walk to Lizzie and Seb's and despite the freezing temperature, I felt a warm glow as Oliver took my hand.

"I don't know what you put in Granddad's tea," Oliver said. "But he hasn't made one single complaint since your visit. And he's taking this Santa gig very seriously."

I laughed. "Maybe he's enjoying doing something useful. Something fun, even."

"Well, whatever the reason is," Oliver said. "Thank you." He stopped walking and while Frank took the opportunity to have a good sniff at the ground, Oliver took both my hands in his. "For asking him. Granddad can be such a grumpy old so-and-so, he's the last person people usually turn to for help."

Oliver's expression was full of appreciation and the love for his grandfather undeniable. As was my attraction to the man before me. My gaze went from his intense green eyes to his soft tender lips and as he drew me near, butterflies didn't just flutter in my tummy, they flapped and flitted all the way up into my chest cavity. Letting go of my hands, Oliver pulled me into a gentle embrace and brought his face closer to mine and as we began to kiss, the world around us seemed to disappear. It was just him and me.

Frank let out a short sharp bark, bringing me back to reality and our kiss to a reluctant end. I pulled back and smiled at Oliver, just as something cold and wet landed on my nose. I looked around to see huge thick snowflakes falling all about us, while Frank jumped up and down trying to catch them in his mouth.

"Merry Christmas," Oliver said, with a smile.

He took my hand again and as we continued walking in companionable silence, I relished the calm around me. Refusing to think about what Oliver and I were getting into, I was determined to enjoy what time I had left in the village.

As we passed the shop, we both glanced in the window to see Lewis and Marianne perched on stools either side of the counter. Lewis talked with his hands as much as he did with his mouth, while Marianne threw her head back and laughed at whatever it was Lewis had just said. I smiled as Oliver did a double take.

"Did you see that?" Oliver shook his head as if he couldn't believe his eyes.

"I did," I replied. I wore a knowing expression as we crossed the road and headed for a terrace of cottages similar to Bluebell Row.

"Please don't tell me you had a hand in that too?" Oliver asked.

I grinned.

"You're incredible. You know that?"

While I chuckled in response, Oliver slowed in his step, eventually bringing me to a standstill with him. Gone was his smile. Oliver held my gaze, his face earnest. "Stay," he said. "Don't go back to London."

Oliver had previously joked about me stopping on in Little Leatherington, but unlike then, on this occasion he seemed serious. I let out a nervous laugh.

He took both my hands in his for a second time. "I'd like to get to know you more. For you to get to know me more."

Don't say I didn't warn you, said my brain.

Tell him yes, of course you'll stay! said my heart.

"Oliver, I..."

Seb's voice suddenly rang out, interrupting the moment. "Antonia!" he said, racing out of his front door and towards us. "It's Christmas Eve."

Forced to tear my eyes away from Oliver's, I let go of his hands and plastered a smile on my face. "It certainly is, young man. So why aren't you in bed already?"

CHAPTER 42

*S*eb clearly didn't care about the cold or the snow and I shook my head and giggled at the sight of him charging towards us in his blue pyjamas, red fleecy dressing gown, and tiger head slippers. I couldn't deny how cute the little boy looked and with his hair wet and brushed back off his face, it was evident he wasn't long out of the bath. "We thought we'd come and say Merry Christmas," I said.

He slowed in his step, his eyes narrowing as he neared us. "Who are you?" he asked Oliver, his expression a mix of curiosity and suspicion.

Oliver crouched down to Seb's level. "I'm Ollie." He held out his hand by way of a formal introduction. "Pleased to meet you at last."

As Seb accepted the gesture, he seemed to give Oliver the once-over, before turning his attention to me. "Antonia?"

"Yes," I replied.

"You never said *you* had a special friend too."

I bit down on my lips, not sure how to respond.

"You told me all your friends were in London."

"Sebastian, what are you doing?" Lizzie's voice resounded from the house. "Get back inside this minute."

I smiled at Lizzie's annoyance and the use of her son's Sunday name.

"You're going to catch your death out there."

As Seb looked at Oliver again, he slowly shook his head and sighed. "Women," he said. He turned and doing as he was told, moseyed back towards his front door.

Oliver rose to his feet, clearly amused by the little boy. But I could see his mind was still on our conversation. "I'm not giving up," he said, smiling. "Please, just think about it."

The last time I'd been asked to think about something, I'd ended up being roped into hosting Christmas lunch. "Oliver," I said. "It's..."

"Did you know...?" a familiar voice interrupted.

I looked round to see Jason coming towards us.

"...that every Christmas Eve in Caracas, people don't just go to church any old how? They roller-skate there."

I smiled, knowing if Jason had told me that when I'd first met him, I wouldn't have believed a word of it.

"It's a tradition so popular, that roads across the whole city are closed so that everyone can skate to church in safety."

Oliver laughed. "Now that I'd love to see."

Jason lowered his voice to a whisper. "I take it you're here to see Santa as well?"

"Who else?" I said.

Oliver smiled. He held an arm out, indicating I should lead the way. "After you, special friend," he said. He gave me a wink, for which I gave him a playful nudge.

As we reached the door, Lizzie herded us all inside. "Here, let me take your coats."

Unlike at Aunt Lillian's, there was no stepping into a hallway. The front entrance of Lizzie's cottage opened straight into its living room. The space was cosy and warm courtesy of the small wood burner in the chimney breast, and serene, I noted, thanks to the neutrals and beiges it was decorated in. Even the Christmas tree adornments were of the same palette and taking in the room's neatness, I couldn't help but wonder how she kept it so immaculate with a young child.

"Please, sit down, everyone," Lizzie said. "I'll get you all a drink."

Seb sat on the deep, squidgy cream sofa. He was barefooted, I noticed, and his slippers lay on top of the wood burner, no doubt, drying after he'd worn them outside in the snow. His eyes lit up as soon as he saw Jason. "Have you come to wish us a Merry Christmas too?" he asked, excited by everyone's presence.

"I have," Jason replied. He took the seat next to Seb, while Oliver and I settled on an armchair each. "Are you all ready for tomorrow?" Jason asked.

"I am," Seb replied, confident.

I smiled as the little boy jumped onto his feet and ran to a little side table, drawing everyone's attention to the plate sat on it. "These are for Santa," he said, pointing to a glass of milk and a mince pie. "And this is for Rudolph." He indicated a huge carrot. "Rudolph is my favourite reindeer."

"What's this about?" Jason said. He picked up a children's book that lay on the coffee table, before making a show of studying the cover. "*The Night Before Christmas*. Ooh, this is a good one."

Seb's eyes widened. "And that's my bestest Christmas story," he said, taking the book and having a look at it himself. "Would you like me to read it to you?"

Lizzie reappeared with a tray of mugs. "Hot chocolate, anyone?"

"Thank you," Oliver said to Lizzie, reaching for a cup.

As Lizzie held her tray towards me so I, too, could take a drink, she smirked and discreetly nodded in Oliver's direction.

Taking a mug from her, I pursed my lips and rolled my eyes.

Seb looked to Lizzie. "Mummy, look at all these new friends." His eyes went from her, to me, to Oliver, and to Jason, while each of us smiled back at him. "We've gone from knowing no one to knowing *everyone*. This really is the best Christmas ever." Turning to the first page in his book, he shook his head, as if unable to believe his good fortune.

Lizzie's eyes teared up as she took in her son's delight. Her gaze turned to me. "Thank you," she said, discreetly mouthing her words.

No sooner had he started reading, than Seb had stopped. "What's that?" he asked, as if confused.

"I can't hear anything," Oliver said.

"Me neither," I said.

While the rest of us pretended not to know what the little boy was talking about, Seb cocked his head at the sound of jingling bells, alongside a vague rumbling. His gaze went to the window. "It seems to be coming from out there." He got up to look and cupping his eyes, he pressed his face to the glass. Colourful lights flashed into the room. "Mummy, you have to come and see this," he said, his voice loud and clear.

As Seb ran to the door and threw it open, Oliver hastily pulled out his phone and nodded at Lizzie to let her know he was recording.

"Mummy, it's Santa. On his sleigh. Being pulled by a big red tractor."

Such was his excitement, as he jumped up and down, I thought the little boy might hyperventilate.

"I think he might have come to see us."

"*Ho! Ho! Ho!*" Ted said, his voice easily louder than the bells and engine noise.

Oliver positioned himself outside to get the best view of Seb who stood in the doorway, while Lizzie, Jason and I were able to watch freely. I bit down on my lips as I clocked Barrowboy behind the tractor's steering wheel. Surprised to see him involved at all, I couldn't believe he'd agreed to wear a green elf suit. He had to be the most serious Santa's little helper I'd ever seen. Unlike Ted, I noted, who was faultless in his role. His smile couldn't have been bigger as he waved from the back of an attached sheep trailer that had been made up to look like a sleigh.

"Isn't this great," Jason said, ruffling Seb's hair.

"It sure is," the little boy replied. He went from jumping to hopping, going from one foot to the other. "Look! Look! Santa's little helper is getting out."

Forced to keep his head down thanks to the huge snowflakes that fell thick and fast, Barrowboy descended from the tractor's cab. I could see he was trying to get into character as he unhooked the rear of the trailer. However, trying to negotiate the weather as he worked made him look more pained than perky, unlike Ted, who continued to enjoy his role. The old man picked up a huge Christmas present and walked down the ramp.

Taking in the brightly coloured wrapping paper, I wondered what was in the box. I certainly hadn't provided a gift for Seb. My heart melted, as Ted gave me a discreet nod, and realising he'd taken it upon himself to provide one, it was all I could do to stop myself throwing my arms around him.

"Is that little Seb whom I see," Ted said, as he began making his way towards the door. "I've been looking for you."

Seb stood there in awe. "Mummy, he *is* coming to see us. He even knows my name."

I smiled at Ted as he approached, knowing I couldn't have asked for a better Father Christmas and not just because he came bearing gifts. Of course, Ted already had the necessary hair and beard, but his red suit with its white furry cuffs, thick black belt, and big silver buttons was equally perfect. Finishing his outfit with a pair of black lace-up boots, Ted had even given his cheeks a rosy glow with smudges of lipstick.

"I'm here to make an extra special visit, with an extra special present," Ted said.

Seb's jaw dropped at the size of the box. "That's for me?"

Ted laughed loudly. "Yes, it's for you." Ted gestured to the rest of us. "From all your new friends here."

Seb swallowed as he looked at each one of us for a second time. "Thank you," he said, his voice suddenly mouse-like as he accepted his gift, "so much."

I could see Seb had tears in his eyes and I heard Lizzie's breath catch before she put a hand up to cover her mouth. Placing my arm around her shoulder, I gave her a comforting squeeze.

"And thank you, Santa. For bringing it to me."

As the little boy looked from his gift to Ted, my eyes went from them to Lizzie, Jason, and Oliver. It seemed we were all a bit teary, and I'd have put money on me not being the only one with a lump in my throat.

"Did you bring Rudolph with you?" Seb asked, hopeful.

"Not this time," Ted replied. "He needs as much rest as he can get before our big journey tonight."

Seb nodded and took a much-needed deep breath. "I understand."

"But if you promise to be a good boy throughout the coming year, maybe I'll bring him to see you next Christmas."

"Really?" Seb said, his eyes widening.

As did mine. How Ted planned on getting his hands on a reindeer was anyone's guess.

"Really," Ted replied. He smiled at the little boy. "Now you go and put your present under that tree." He pointed to the inside of Lizzie's cottage. "Because it's nearly your bedtime and I have to go."

"Can't you stay a bit longer?" Seb asked, almost desperate. "We have hot chocolate. See?" He pointed into the lounge, at Lizzie's tray on the coffee table.

"And risk not delivering my presents on time?" Ted opened his arms to give Seb a hug before leaving.

Seb raced into the house, dropped his gift under the tree and grabbing his slippers off the wood burner, he frantically put them on before running back to the doorway and throwing himself into Ted's embrace. He closed his eyes tight.

Seeing the two of them was such a heart-warming sight and as I looked to Oliver, I was pleased to see he was still filming.

"Come on now, Seb," Lizzie said. "It's time for Santa to go."

Seb stepped back. "I love you, Santa," he said.

Ted stood there, as if lost for words.

Seb looked up at his mum. "I wish Daddy could have been here."

I took in Lizzie's sadness. "I know, sweetie," she said.

Watching the two of them, I thought my heart would break too.

CHAPTER 43

Christmas Day

*T*he sound of my phone alarm slowly forced its way
through to my brain, but, not ready to wake up, I
refused to acknowledge it. On and on the ringing went until
finally the noise properly broke through and as I flung my arm
out and grabbed my mobile to silence it, I felt tempted to hit the
snooze button. I knew I couldn't. I had a Christmas Day
schedule to follow. I shot up in bed, as the words *Christmas* and
Day hit me.

I threw the bedcovers back and swung my legs over the side
of the mattress. As I shoved my feet into my slippers, I checked
the time. Having managed to ignore my alarm for a whole
twenty minutes, I consoled myself in the knowledge that I wasn't
that much off-track. "Come on, Frank," I said, grabbing my
dressing gown and putting it on. "Wakey wakey."

I paused to admire the dress I planned to wear hanging on
the back of the door. It was a black woollen fitted number and at

calf length would look great with the only footwear I had: my trusty Dr Martens. Having decided that if I was entertaining the only way to do it was in style, I looked up to the heavens and smiled. "Thanks, Aunt Lillian," I said, hoping she didn't mind me borrowing it.

Leaving the dress behind, I made my way straight down to the kitchen and checking my notes, the first thing on my list was to get the turkey out of the fridge so it could come up to room temperature. As I heaved the foil-covered roasting tray out and placed it on the counter, I felt determined to make my Christmas lunch one to remember. Not least for Seb and Lizzie. I recalled the little boy's sadness because his dad hadn't been present to experience Santa's special visit. His father's absence clearly still played on his mind and if my contribution to Seb's day helped ease that, then I'd be one happy woman.

I smiled as I picked up my pen and ticked off the first of my to-dos. With a while to go before the turkey went in the oven, I told myself I could relax for a bit. "Next up," I said. "Fire. Then coffee."

Having cleaned the hearth and got the open fire ablaze, I set about making my drink, all the while pondering my time in Little Leatherington. Looking back, I couldn't believe how much my plans had changed. In the space of a couple of weeks I'd gone from being determined to lock myself away for the festive duration, to organising a group Christmas lunch. I chuckled. We were such a varied bunch and picturing us all around the dinner table, I imagined lively conversations abound. In my head, even Barrowboy joined in.

My phone bleeped and picking it up, my tummy tickled at the sight of Oliver's name and wondering what he wanted, I clicked to read his incoming text.

Happy Christmas morning. Granddad says he's looking forward to lunch. I'm just looking forward to seeing you x

Wrapped in a warm glow and resting my phone against my chin, I grinned, knowing I looked forward to seeing Oliver in return. *A bit too much*, I acknowledged, remembering his suggestion that I stay on in the village so we could get to know each other more.

I couldn't deny I felt tempted. I didn't just find Oliver physically attractive, he seemed to have the personality to match. He was fun and he didn't run a mile when I did something embarrassing or got things wrong. Rather than judge or pay lip-service to my less than conventional ideas for earning a living, he seemed supportive and encouraging. I had to admit he was the first man I could actually see myself in a relationship with, in goodness knew how long, which begged the question of what was stopping me from hanging around.

I knew setting up my new business could be done just as easily in the Yorkshire Dales as it could in London. And as I looked out of the window in contemplation, I couldn't help but scoff as my eyes settled on the stone building at the far end of the garden. In Little Leatherington, I didn't even have to think about storage and workshop space. Moreover, with Jules looking to rent out Number 3, I was a ready-made tenant. On the face of it, a life in Little Leatherington held everything I could hope for.

I let out a laugh. If only things were that easy.

All I'd ever known was life in the city and London wasn't just my home, it was the place where I was born and raised. It was where my best friend lived. I pictured my small yet perfectly formed flat and having spent years turning it into my own cosy little abode, I wasn't sure I could give it up. Of course, there were other considerations to bear in mind. London had coffee shops and wine bars and cinemas and takeaways... the list went on. Plus, I didn't exactly have the temperament for country living. If getting stuck up a mountain and mistaking a cow for a burglar proved anything, it was that.

Deciding I had too much to think about already, I left my head and my heart to continue battling it out in silence, while I got on with more important things, like enjoying Christmas.

Frank trotted into the room, no doubt, ready for his breakfast and as per our usual routine, I moved to let him out into the garden, ready to fill his bowl. Opening the back door, however, I immediately froze at the sight that met me. "What the...?" I said. Faced with a white wall of snow, it seemed no one was going anywhere.

I recalled the previous evening's humongous snowflakes swirling around, realising I should have known they'd cause a problem, especially when I remembered all the times London had been brought to a standstill by a couple of inches of snow. As I laughed at my naivety, I picked up my phone and took a photo of the doorway to send to Jules, knowing she'd love it.

Appreciating that the house wasn't really buried under a solid twenty feet of snow and that I was more than likely looking at a snowdrift, I wondered how best to tackle it. Another huge grin crossed my face when, after a moment, I came up with the perfect method of demolition. Before I knew it, I was racing upstairs, throwing on some clothes, and hastily searching for my boots. Heading into the kitchen again, I stared at my target and taking a few steps back, I began counting down. "Three, two, one..." I said. Setting off on a run, I charged straight at the wall before me.

Landing in a heap at the other side, I burst into a fit of laughter. I couldn't remember the last time I'd done something so childish and as Frank raced out to join me, my merriment only continued when I struggled to stop him licking my face. I had to clamber onto all fours before I could, at last, get back onto my feet.

I spotted a neighbour looking down at me from her upstairs window and going off her frown, the sight of me bursting out of the kitchen, at that time of the morning, on Christmas Day wasn't as fun an experience for her as it was me. I put my hand up and waved, but rather than return the gesture, the woman shook her head and promptly disappeared. I found myself giggling some more, surprised to find I didn't actually care what the woman thought. For the first time in forever, I didn't care what *anyone* thought. I felt free and joyful and taking in the crisp untouched snow around me, I knew exactly what I wanted to do next.

CHAPTER 44

I lay in the garden, flat on my back, my arms and legs aching from the numerous snow angels I'd made. A few weeks ago, if someone had told me that that was what I'd be doing come Christmas morning, I'd have said they were talking rubbish. My smile faded a little, as I wondered why that would have been my response. Staring up at the sky, I tried to pinpoint when it was that I'd stopped enjoying the simplest of things. When I'd become so boring.

I'd never been a particularly outgoing individual. As a child, I stuck out for being the poor kid and I quickly learned how to shrink into the background. I stayed on the edge, watching and listening rather than trying to join in. Most young people would hate being in that position, but for me, it turned out to be a good thing. I learned from other people's mistakes without having to experience a lot of the angst that most of my contemporaries went through. There was no peer pressure because I didn't mix. My only real friend had been Jules, so I got to be my own person, with my own views.

However, as with most things in life, there was a downside too. In answer to my questions, I'd probably always been boring.

Living a near solitary life with not much money wasn't actually all that fun a lot of the time. To the point that over the years I'd probably forgotten how to enjoy myself. Even when mum died and I no longer had to think so hard about money, I carried on living in the same lacklustre way. I scoffed. The one thing Mum had made sure not to skimp on was her life insurance. As if, if anything happened to her, she hadn't wanted me to be sad *and* penniless. "Sorry, Mum," I said, looking up to the heavens. I might not have squandered her money, but in some ways, I'd definitely wasted the opportunity she'd given me.

Heavy snow began to fall again and with both me and Frank already soaked, I knew it was time to go in. Heading back to the house, I looked up at the neighbouring window to see my audience had doubled. The woman had obviously fetched her partner to see the eccentric visitor staying next door and I smiled and waved at them as they continued to observe me. "You should try it," I said, calling up to them. Of course, while they might not have appreciated my efforts, I knew Seb would and I glanced up at the myriad snowflakes, thinking that later, maybe he and I could build a snowman. "Come on, Frank," I said, grabbing a towel to dry him off as we stepped inside.

With lots to do, I told myself it was time to be an adult again and turning on the hot tap, I hoped the warm water would bring some sensation back to my numb fingers. Drying my hands, I scanned my schedule notes to see that thanks to my garden antics, I'd fallen behind even further. Not only should I have switched on the cooker to heat up, by then the turkey was meant to be well on its way to cooking. I insisted it wasn't a problem, and refusing to worry about it, set the correct oven temperature and placed the roasting tray on the rack inside. We'd just have to eat a bit later than planned. Then I hastily headed out of the room so I could at least be washed and dressed before my guests arrived.

After being out in the cold for so long, getting out of my wet clothes and into a hot steaming bath felt bliss. Although as I quickly shampooed my hair and soaped up my skin, I couldn't help but smile. Despite throwing my timetable into disarray, I'd enjoyed the best Christmas morning I'd had in years. I understood why, of course. London wasn't exactly set up for frolicking in the snow first thing. At least, my bit of London wasn't, what with me living in a second-floor flat, on a busy road, with no garden. I giggled at the prospect of ringing Jules to tell her what I'd been up to, knowing she probably wouldn't believe me.

Climbing out, I wrapped myself in a towel and made my way to the bedroom. Taking a seat at the dressing table, I prepared to dry my hair. As I split it into sections, I pondered the day ahead. I could catch up on my to-do list, I decided. This year really was going to be the Christmas to beat all Christmases.

Switching on the hairdryer, I again pictured me and my guests all chatting and laughing as we tucked into our meal. I saw plates of succulent turkey, golden crispy roast potatoes, glazed carrots, and pigs in blankets. All with cranberry sauce and covered in lashings of rich meaty gravy. As if that wasn't enough, my mouth watered at the thought of the fruit-filled Christmas pudding and brandy cream that awaited us. There were mince pies and slices of Christmas cake for those who had room, not forgetting Jules's special recipe gingerbread trifle. My stomach rumbled and pushing all thoughts of food to one side, I continued to dry my hair. Focusing, it wasn't long before I got lost in the white noise.

The room suddenly fell silent and realising the hairdryer had abruptly stopped working, I frowned, wondering what was wrong with it. I turned it off and back on again in the hope of it restarting. But it was to no avail and tapping the end of the nozzle, I tried the button once more. My brow creased even further as I stared at the damn thing, unable to believe that out of all the times it could have broken down, it had to choose then. I reached under the dressing table and pulled out its plug, before slotting the pins into the adjacent socket. However, pressing the on button yet again, I continued to be met with silence.

Questioning if its fuse had gone, I caught sight of the window reflecting in the mirror in front of me. My heart sank as I rose from my seat and went to look out. I took in the heavy snow fall, seeing that my snow angels had all but disappeared. Huge fat flakes fell thick and fast. Severe weather was known to play havoc with power lines and I turned to look at the hairdryer. Realising the problem wasn't the fuse at all, any confidence I had about the day ahead instantly vanished.

With half my hair still in sections, I spun on my heels and raced down to the kitchen. Heading straight for the oven, I prayed it would be hot, but as I opened the appliance door, there was no sudden blast of heat. My shoulders slumped as I stared at the roasting tray, hardly daring to pull back the foil that covered the turkey. I winced. "Oh Lordy," I said, reaching for the silver to reveal nothing but raw meat.

My breath caught in my throat as I realised that Jason and Barrowboy wouldn't be properly celebrating their first Christmas since their parents had died. That Seb would remember his first Christmas without his dad as the Christmas he was made to starve. That Lizzie would be left to pick up the pieces should her son have a hunger-induced meltdown. And that Oliver and Ted would be muddling through more than ever that year.

Thanks to a power cut, Christmas was ruined.

CHAPTER 45

The clock was ticking and I didn't have time for a pity party. I slammed the oven door shut and rose to my feet. I picked up my phone off the counter and clicked to video call Jules, knowing that if anyone could salvage the situation, it would be her. "Come on, come on," I said, hoping for a few words of wisdom as I waited for her face to appear on the screen. The ringing tone continued. She wasn't picking up.

My shoulders slumped. Of course, she wasn't. Thanks to our Christmas swap she was taking things easy that year. Unlike me, she had no guests to consider and was, no doubt, having a long lie-in, with Harry making her breakfast in bed. I told myself to let them enjoy their leisurely morning and that I'd been relying on Jules far too much of late. It was time to stand on my own two feet. Whatever the day threw at me, I was more than capable of handling everything.

Ending the call, I drummed my fingers on the kitchen top as my brain tried to figure out what to do next. My eyes landed on the numerous notes I'd made, and I scoffed. Were it not for that schedule, I'd have at least been able to wrap a few spuds in tinfoil, throw them on the lounge's open fire and serve up baked potatoes. As it was, in my desire to be organised, I'd none left. They'd all been parboiled and had a good fluffing up.

Exiting the room, I told myself I could be worrying about nothing. For all I knew, the power cut could be peculiar to Aunt Lillian's alone. With no clue where the cottage's fuse box was housed, I rushed upstairs to throw on some clothes again, before heading back down to the front door and stepping outside. "Wow," I said. As my eyes widened at the scene that met me, I didn't think I'd ever seen so much snow.

Trudging down the garden path, snowflakes fell all around me. I struggled to see where the pathway ended and the road began. Drifts had built up against doors, and rooftops were covered, inches thick. My heart sank as I scanned the neighbouring houses. There wasn't a single twinkling Christmas tree light in sight. I filled my cheeks with cold air and slowly exhaled. Taking in the scene once more, all it needed was a strong wind and the village would be in the midst of a blizzard. No wonder there'd been a power cut.

Again, I tried to reassure myself, insisting that just because Bluebell Row had suffered an outage, that didn't mean the entire village had and as such, I could potentially use someone else's oven. Supposing there was only one way to find out, I made my way back inside. Closing the door behind me, I headed straight to the kitchen and picking up my phone for a second time, I dialled Lizzie's number.

"Not you too?" she said, immediately upon answering.

I closed my eyes for a second, my hopes dashed. "I'm afraid so," I said, trying to sound positive.

"I'm sure it won't last long," Lizzie said to the sound of Seb playing in the background. "I shouldn't think the electricity board will want to let customers down on Christmas Day."

"You're right," I replied. "There'd be a riot if they did." Although I didn't have a clue what I would feed everyone if the energy supply didn't come back. I couldn't give my guests a hot cup of tea, let alone Christmas lunch with all the trimmings.

After ending the call, I made my way into the living room where Frank lay peacefully in front of the fire, clearly immune to the turmoil I felt. Plonking myself down on a chair, I took in the table before me. Tempted to grab a bottle of wine to drown my sorrows, the crystal glasses might still be operative, but with no food to serve, the perfectly laid crockery and shiny silverware had been rendered useless. I couldn't even send for takeaway. Unlike in London where every type of food going could be ordered with one quick swipe on a phone, Little Leatherington's nearest restaurant was miles away and considering the weather, even if I could organise delivery, I'd have put money on the village being cut-off. I rested my chin in my hand. Gone were the pictures of us all sat around enjoying a magnificent lunch. The best I could offer were peanut butter sandwiches and a slice of Christmas cake. I sighed, hoping none of my guests had a nut allergy.

I thought back to how happy I'd been that morning. Cavorting around in the back garden making snow angels. As I sat there at that table though, my feelings couldn't have been more opposite and not for the first time since landing in Little Leatherington, I wanted to scurry back to London. The power cut wasn't my fault, but I couldn't help but feel I'd let everyone down.

I told myself I was being self-indulgent and that there had to be something I could do, even if that meant standing outside for hours barbequing the damn turkey. Which would have been an option had I seen an actual barbeque hanging around Number 3, Bluebell Row. Having had more than a good scout about the place, that seemed to be the one and only item Jules's Aunt Lillian didn't have. I sat up straight, realising I had seen something else that might be of use.

he gave me a lingering kiss. "There's a lot you don't know about me," he said. "If you think my abilities in the kitchen are impressive..." He kissed me again. "You want to see me in the bedroom."

Not doubting his claim for one second, if I didn't have guests due, I'd have been tempted to forget all caution and lead the man upstairs there and then. I pressed my hips against his, suddenly aware that he'd have let me too. I smiled.

"And that's just one of the reasons you should stay," he said.

Telling myself Oliver wasn't the only one who could be a tease, I went in for another kiss. "Let's just say I'm still thinking about it," I said, before quickly letting go of him. I headed to the fridge and pulled out the big bowl of potatoes, smiling in the knowledge that they weren't the only things that were parboiled and fluffed up. I handed them to Oliver. "In the meantime, if you chop these up into rectangles for me." I took a knife out of the cutlery drawer and held it out for him to take.

Oliver laughed. "Your wish is my command."

Observing him roll up his shirt sleeves and get to work, I felt torn. Oliver made staying on in Little Leatherington sound so easy. But it was all right for him. He wasn't the one being asked to uproot his life. Then again, as I pictured the property agents I'd dealt with down in London, with their shiny shoes and slick patter, even if Oliver had offered to make the move instead, I appreciated he would never fit in. He wouldn't be happy.

"It's a risk for both of us," he said, as if reading my mind. Oliver turned to look at me. "But in my view, some things are worth it."

I picked up the carrier bag and began emptying it of its contents, neatly lining up the jars of paprika, cayenne pepper, oregano, thyme and dried onion and making sure they were perfectly straight, I told myself that that was the problem. I wasn't one for taking chances. When it came to people in general, I didn't trust easily and while I knew in many ways I was quirky, unconventional, and could speak my mind, when it came to matters of the heart, I was an all or nothing woman. Having seen the damage done when relationships didn't work out, I was convinced mum never really got over the fact that dad left us without a second glance. And like Lizzie had pointed out when talking about her own situation, she wasn't the only one left holding the baby; there were millions of single parents out there. Oliver might not have been talking about us starting a family, but I still hoped to become a mum one day. So while Oliver might have been right in his words, I couldn't help but question if he'd be saying the same thing in six months' time, let alone six years. Or by then, would he be taking a *risk* on someone else?

Oliver put his knife down and taking the carrier bag off me, twisted me round to face him. "Whatever this is, whatever's going on between us, I'm not going to put pressure on it. If that means taking things slowly and doing things long distance until we figure it all out, then count me in. I'm not going anywhere. Unless you want me to?"

Standing there, I couldn't bring myself to reply one way or the other.

Oliver kissed me on the forehead. "Look, why don't you go and get yourself ready? Everyone will be here soon. Tell me what we're having, and I can get started."

I picked up my phone and showed Oliver the recipe.

His eyes widened and he let out a laugh. "You're joking." He looked over at all the spices. "I thought we were having a curry."

I chuckled, glad of the light relief. "When it comes to me and cooking, I assure you, simple is best."

"Okay, then," Oliver said, continuing to smile as he got back to his chopping. "Deep fried turkey and chips it is."

CHAPTER 47

*A*s we all sat there in our Christmas cracker crowns, it didn't seem to matter that a traditional lunch hadn't been served. To say I'd been worried about how the day would go, everyone present seemed happy and content.

"This is the best Christmas dinner ever," Seb said. Holding yet another piece of fried turkey in one hand, he stuffed a ketchup-soaked chip into his mouth with the other.

Lizzie laughed. "Well that's me let off basting duties next year." She looked my way. "This really is lovely, Antonia," she said of our meal. "If we were round at mine, we'd be on jam sandwiches."

I laughed. "Don't think that didn't cross my mind. Although I can't take all the credit." I felt Oliver place a hand on my knee. "I had plenty of assistance."

"If I didn't know any better, I'd think we were in Japan," Jason said.

While everyone fell silent, as if wondering what the man was talking about, Barrowboy shook his head and rolled his eyes.

Jason was obviously about to treat us to another random Christmas fact and smiling at his brother's response, I had to wonder how many times he had, in fact, been forced to listen to Jason's Yuletide ramblings. I, on the other hand, grinned, more than happy to hear his latest offering. For me, the day wouldn't have been the same had Jason not mentioned at least one far off Christmas tradition.

"What are you talking about?" Ted asked. "This village is nothing like Japan."

"No, but this is," Jason replied. He pointed to his dinner. "Did you know that Christmas lunch in Japan is actually KFC?"

While Seb and I accepted his every word, I could see the others were sceptical.

"Honestly," Jason carried on. "In 1974, KFC Japan came up with the advertising slogan *kurisumasu ni wa kentakkii*, which means *Kentucky for Christmas*. And Takeshi Okawara, the manager of the only KFC store in the country at that time, began selling party barrels, claiming they were a proper Christmas tradition. Which is funny because they don't officially celebrate Christmas over there. Anyway, it took off and even now 3.6 million people sit down to eat KFC on Christmas Day."

"Really?" Ted asked, amazed.

Jason nodded.

"Well I didn't know that."

"Jason knows lots about Christmas," Seb said to Ted. "Don't you, Jason?"

"Well, tradition or not, I can't eat another thing," Ted said. He patted his belly. "I'm stuffed."

"You can't say that," Seb said. "You haven't had any Christmas pudding yet."

As everyone laughed and began talking about their own special festive traditions, I was happy to sit and listen. Having spent year after year locking myself away, it wasn't as if I had anything interesting to contribute.

The wine flowed as Ted and Oliver regaled everyone with

stories about Mrs Sharples. Jason and Barrowboy had everyone roaring with laughter when it came to their parents. And to ensure her son wasn't reminded of his father's absence, Lizzie dropped the previous night's Santa visit into the conversation which sent Seb's excited chatter into overdrive.

I hoped I wasn't tempting fate, but watching the four of them, Lizzie, Seb, Jason and Barrowboy already looked like a little family and turning my attention to Oliver and Ted, I wondered if, deep down, we had what it took to make a family of our own too.

While my head said no and my heart said yes, I knew even if I went back to London, there were changes afoot. Jules and Harry were expecting their first child, so didn't need me in the way. And while I had the excitement of setting up my new business to keep me busy, all work and no play may have been good enough prior to me landing in Little Leatherington, but I couldn't say that still stood. I looked round at my guests once more, aware that if I did go back to the city, I'd miss each and every one of them. I smiled. Including Barrowboy.

But it wasn't about them. Or about Oliver. Or about Jules. Whether I stayed in Little Leatherington or not was about me. I recalled my morning's musings about the wasted opportunity Mum had given me. I thought about the little girl who imagined her horse on the merry-go-round breaking free. I pictured myself stuck up Fotherghyll Fell, working out my funeral numbers and realising I hadn't left a single mark on the world around me.

I suddenly felt overwhelmed and seeing everyone had stopped eating, seized the chance to grab a moment to myself. I rose to my feet and not wanting to interrupt everyone's gaiety, I discretely gathered a few plates and carried them out to the kitchen. Placing them in the sink, I struggled to get my head around the predicament I found myself in. I was way out of my comfort zone yet at the same time I'd never felt so comfortable. Talk about weird.

And scary, I acknowledged.

It was as if I didn't know myself anymore. As if Little Leatherington had waved a magic festive wand and turned me into someone else. The real Antonia Styles wasn't a people person. No way would she host Christmas lunch. Let alone have the confidence to look after someone else's child. She certainly wouldn't play matchmaker for Lewis and Marianne, or, fingers crossed, give Barrowboy and Lizzie a little nudge in the right direction. As for making the grumpiest old man in the village smile and helping the biggest Christmas fan on the planet celebrate again, there was no chance. Most important of all, the real Antonia wouldn't fall in love.

There. I'd admitted it.

Oliver suddenly appeared in the doorway. "Everything all right?" he asked.

Pulling myself together, I turned on the hot tap and began filling the sink with water. "Fine," I replied, as I added a big squirt of washing-up liquid. From the corner of my eye, I saw Oliver step forward. I sensed he was about to say something. "Yes!" I said, before he got the chance.

"Sorry?"

I turned to face him. "Yes. I'll stay."

At first, he looked confused, as if he wasn't quite sure what I was referring to. But his smile grew as my words sank in and he took another step towards me.

My heart raced as he suddenly pulled me to him. He placed his hands on my waist, before lifting me straight off the ground. I squealed as he spun me around, before, at last, planting my feet back down on terra firma.

His expression came over all serious. "You're sure about this?" he asked. "About us?"

Smiling, I nodded. His arms wrapped around me and as I found myself lost in the most perfect of kisses, I knew more than ever that I'd made the right decision.

"Oh no," a little boy's voice said.

Our lips separated, and unable to take our eyes off each other, Oliver and I giggled at the interruption.

"There's a delay on the Christmas pudding, everyone," Seb said, making a hasty retreat. "And don't go into the kitchen. Those two are kissing."

A cheer erupted in the living room, making me and Oliver laugh even more.

"I suppose we should get it over with," Oliver said.

As Oliver took my hand, ready to lead me into the fracas, I held back.

"What is it?"

I thought about the one person without whom none of what was happening would have been possible. "There's someone I need to speak to first."

Oliver looked at me inquisitively.

I picked up my phone and clicked to video call Jules. "You think that was loud," I said, indicating the crowd in the living room. "Get ready to cover your ears."

THE END

ACKNOWLEDGEMENTS

I'd like to start by thanking everyone at Bloodhound Books. Especially Betsy, Fred, my editor, Clare, Tara, Maria and Shirley. You're a great team to work with and here's to a fabulous new chapter in the Bloodhound story.

A special thank you goes to Jonty Rhodes and Jo Wulf of the Cave Rescue Organisation. Not only for the work you and your team do in the real world, but for talking me through how you'd help Antonia in her fictional one. Antonia's mountainside calamity was such fun to write, but without your help I wouldn't have known where to start when it came to saving her. As you both know, left to my own devices there'd have been helicopters galore! I'd also like to thank you for making me aware of the Umbles. I hope I did them justice on the page.

I'd like to say thanks to Jenny O'Brien, nurse and crime writer extraordinaire. My knowledge of the human skeleton has always been a bit sketchy and before talking to you the only leg bone I could have named was the femur. Not only do I now know where to find the tibia and fibula, I can spell them too. I can't wait for these to come up in a pub quiz.

Because farming would never make my list of specialist

subjects either, my next thank you goes to Louise and Anthony Crisp. Without your expertise, Clarabelle's dairy herd wouldn't have survived the winter.

Finally, I'd like to thank all my readers, without whom I wouldn't be doing the job I love. I hope my stories continue to make you laugh and, at times, cry. And that they take you to the same happy place they take me as I write them.

Here's to a very merry Christmas for all of us.

Suzie x

A NOTE FROM THE PUBLISHER

Thank you for reading this book. If you enjoyed it please do consider leaving a review on Amazon to help others find it too.

We hate typos. All of our books have been rigorously edited and proofread, but sometimes mistakes do slip through. If you have spotted a typo, please do let us know and we can get it amended within hours.

info@bloodhoundbooks.com

Printed in Great Britain
by Amazon